A
HOLIDAY
LOVE AFFAIR

KIRSTEN S. BLACKETER

A HOLIDAY LOVE AFFAIR

Printed in the United States of America.
First Printing, 2020
ISBN: 978-1966905127

Written by Kirsten S. Blacketer.
Published by BlackShip Press
Kirsten.blacketer@gmail.com

https://kirstensblacketer.com

DEDICATION

To my Husband who is Evan in so many ways. I'm your Lucy and your Ben and your Penelope all rolled into one. Sorry you have to deal with that chaos. Thanks for putting up with me.

I love you.

2020 Motto: Embrace the Suck.

A Letter from the Author

Dear Reader,

When I started writing A Lockdown Love Affair, I never anticipated it would spawn a spin off story for Evan and Lucy. I finished A Holiday Love Affair in the hope of life returning to some semblance of normalcy by the end of October, unfortunately this hasn't proven to be the case. This year has been an unexpected whirlwind of disappointment and surprises, and at this point, I'm taking it as it comes and channeling my emotions into writing.

I beg your indulgence as you read. While real events inspired this story, and its predecessor, these books have taken on a life of their own and created their own universe. Please read and enjoy this story with an open mind and an adventurous spirit. I hope you enjoy it just as much as you did A Lockdown Love Affair.

With love,

Kirsten S. Blacketer

P.S. Remember, be kind and love one another.

TABLE OF CONTENTS

Chapter One
The Imaginary Evan

Lucy

October

Today my best friend will marry the man who stole her heart. Fortunately, their wedding will be a simple, uncomplicated affair. Two people, madly in love, with a handful of witnesses and a judge. Over and done in five minutes. Wham, bam, where's the afterparty?

Just like every single one of my relationships.

I wish I could say I love weddings. But I don't. I hate them. Almost as much as I hate holidays. The horrified looks on my friends' faces when I tell them solidifies my distaste.

The underwire of the strapless bra digs into my side and I shift uncomfortably. "Penelope, are you done? Seriously, the car's out front waiting for us."

"Coming!" Penelope's voice echoes down the hallway.

I shift from one foot to the other. These heels are killing me. I'd give anything for my Danskins right now, but I want to look nice for my friend. This is her day. I bite my tongue as the complaint congeals on the tip of it.

Penelope appears in the living room doorway wearing a cream-colored, pin-up style gown with lace trim that accents her dark hair and wide, hopeful eyes. Not a traditional gown by any standard, but it suits her perfectly. She smooths her hand over the loose French braid and along the pearl choker at her throat.

"Do I look okay?" The flutter in her voice betrays her

nerves.

"You're fucking gorgeous." I take her hand in mine and squeeze it. "Now, let's go, or Ben will call Joey to send out a search party."

Her brilliant smile eases the twisting anxiety in my gut. "Thanks for being here with me. I know how much you hate this stuff."

"You're lucky I love you so much." I grin. "Besides, I'm only in this for dinner afterward. Ben did get us reservations at The River Cafe."

"You're ridiculous." Penelope pauses. Her gaze glides over my body. *Here it comes.*

"You look amazing!" She grins and pulls the wool wrap around her shoulders. "I don't think I've ever seen you in a dress before."

"And you probably never will again." I shake my head. "Scrubs are far superior. They let my body breathe!" I pull at the underwire again. "This bra is going to kill me."

"Well, don't take it off until *after* dinner, okay?" Penelope winks and moves toward the door.

"Fine." I stumble, nearly twisting my ankle in these three-inch heels. "Damn it. These things are coming off as soon as I sit my ass down at dinner."

"Deal. It's only going to be the four of us at dinner anyway." Penelope opens the door and the cool October breeze drifts across my skin.

"The infamous Evan will be joining us?" I can't keep the snark from my tone. I've heard Penelope and Ben talk about Evan for months, and yet I've never seen him. Personally, I don't think he exists except as a blurred figure in their imagination.

During the pandemic lockdown and subsequent chaos, I lost myself in work. Six days a week, swing shifts and overtime. Some days I felt dead on my feet. I can only blame myself though. I took every shift they offered me at the hospital, and I didn't stop. I didn't want to. Work keeps me grounded in the midst of all the uncertainty.

Today is the first day I've taken for myself since January, and it's not really for myself. The head nurse practically threw a party when I asked for some time off, even if it was only one day.

"Oh, that's right." Penelope carefully makes her way down the steps of the brownstone. She turns to face me. "You haven't met him yet, have you?"

I shake my head and motion for her to get into the car first. The limo driver nods before closing the door. The leather seats are cool beneath my fingertips. "I still think he's a figment of your imagination."

Penelope laughs. "Just because you haven't met him doesn't mean he's not real."

"If you say so." I inhale deep and eye the mini bar in the center console.

As if reading my mind, Penelope grabs the open bottle of chilled champagne and pours two glasses. "Here. This will take the edge off."

"This is your wedding day, not mine." I accept the glass. "I should be calming your nerves, not the other way around."

"Why would I be nervous?" She laughs and lifts the champagne in a toast. "To us."

"To us." We clink glasses and I down half the shimmering liquid in one swallow. The bubbles tickle my throat. I'm much more of a whisky girl, but the fancy stuff isn't bad.

I'm halfway through my second glass when we pull up in front of the courthouse. I finish the champagne and set the glass aside. "Ready?"

Penelope nods, a huge grin painted on her lips.

When we step from the car, I notice Ben first. His broad shoulders and tall stature make him hard to miss, plus he's handsome as the devil. Penelope's lucky her stalker neighbor was a sexy, eligible bachelor. My heart sinks. Some girls have all the luck.

"Ladies, I was wondering if you'd ever show up." Ben's voice is stern but it echoes with humor. Lucky girl indeed.

"Sorry, I couldn't find my grandma's pearls." Penelope touches the choker at her throat.

"Lucy." Ben acknowledges my presence with a polite nod and a half smile.

"Stalker Ben." I grin at him. "Congratulations."

"Thank you." He turns his head for a brief moment and I follow his gaze.

My heart drops into sinus tachycardia. I press my hand against my sternum and take a deep breath. My mind races. *Calm down. It's a man. It's not like you've never seen one before. Get a grip, girl.*

If Ben were a handsome devil, then this most certainly would be his angelic equivalent. The man smiles and my body bursts into flames. A boyish charm laced with mischief glints in his eyes, but his aura is downright seductive. Boy next door meets sinful fantasy. What the hell? I shake off the unexpected physical reaction and extend my hand.

"Lucy Mackewitz. You must be imaginary Evan." My voice sounds stronger than I feel when I address the man who looks like he stepped out of a *Hugo Boss* advertisement.

He chuckles and grasps my hand in a firm clasp. Damn, he's strong. My gaze rakes over him, from his perfectly kept dirty blond hair, over his broad shoulders, and down to his trim waist. Does he live in the gym? His warmth sinks into me and it takes a tremendous amount self-control not to launch myself at him like a starving beast. *Calm down. This isn't the first time you've been struck by insta-lust. Control your fucking hormones, woman.*

"Evan Waldorf. It's nice to finally meet you, Lucy. Ben and Penelope have told me so much about you." His gleaming smile oozes charm. That crystalline blue gaze holds mine and I swear I see a flash of hunger. Or is it amusement? I shake the thoughts from my mind and force a saccharine smile.

"Of course, they have." I glare at Ben and Penelope who seem riveted at the byplay between me and Evan.

He releases my hand and the immediate pang of loss leaves my brain whiplashed.

"Don't you two have an appointment with the judge in the courtyard?" I ignore the man standing far too close to me and focus on my friend and her soon-to-be husband.

Evan's chuckle makes the hair on my arms prickle with awareness.

As if shaken from a trance, Penelope turns to Ben and pulls his arm. "Come on. Let's get married." He nods and takes her hand. Together they mount the stairs leading to the lovely fountain in front of the historic courthouse.

"Shall we?" Evan's silken baritone wraps around me.

I arch a brow in his direction and note his arm offered in invitation. I can't trust myself to take it. Instead, I pull my coat tighter and follow Penelope and Ben up the stairs.

Evan Waldorf was better left as a blur in my imagination. At least there he wasn't a threat to the vow I'd made years ago, let alone my friendship with Penelope and Ben. *It never ends well.* I remind myself with every step I climb. *Don't encourage him. Just walk away.*

As we approach the judge waiting beside the fountain, I sense Evan's presence and I steel myself a bit more. Damn it, I hate weddings. Is it over yet?

EVAN

OCTOBER

From the moment I saw her, I knew she was the one. Lucy Mackewitz, wrapped in a deep purple coat with her auburn hair tousled and curled, stepped out of the limousine and into my heart.

Outside in the courtyard, the ceremony lasts fifteen minutes. Simple and sweet. Completely appropriate considering Ben hates a big production of anything. He looks at Penelope in a way I've never seen before. Like she's the only person in the world who matters. I'm happy for him.

Truly. He deserves it.

Penelope glows with joy as they make their way down the steps. She looks lovely in her vintage ivory lace gown.

I tuck my hands in my pockets and wait for them to climb into the limo. Lucy comes to a stop beside me. I study her profile, the soft curve of her cheek and aquiline nose. Her rosebud lips purse as she shifts her attention to me.

"It's rude to stare." I can't tell if her tone is sarcastic or condescending. Either way, I prefer a challenge.

"Fine. I won't tell you about the smear of lipstick on your cheek."

Her eyes widen a fraction before she leans down and checks her reflection in the limo window. She scoffs and glares at me over her shoulder.

"After you." I stifle a grin and gesture to the open door.

She huffs and joins Ben and Penelope in the car. I chuckle. She's so easy to rile and this knowledge amuses me. I'm kicking myself it took this long to meet her.

I take my seat beside her and across from Ben and Penelope for the ride to the park. She crosses her arms and leans against the far side of the car. Penelope dominates the conversation as she chatters with excitement. Lucy joins in and slowly the tension eases.

My gaze shifts from Lucy to Ben, who's eyeing me with an unreadable expression. Shit. I have to be careful. He's more observant than most people think.

Ben thinks I fall in love every other month. With every new city I visit, a new girl. He's only partially right. It doesn't take much for a woman to capture my attention. I'm a sucker for a pretty face, and I know it. Penelope thinks I'm a hopeless romantic, but the truth is, I'm lonely and I'm not getting younger. The search is fucking exhausting, and it's not getting easier.

Ever since Ben found Penelope, it's like he's realized life doesn't revolve around work. While that bodes well for everyone at the office, I can't help feel like now Ben's hyper aware of my lack of companionship. I glance at him across the limo. He's distracted by his wife. I bite my tongue and smile. If this wasn't my best friend's wedding, I would think this whole evening was a setup.

We stop at Brooklyn Bridge Park and take some photographs with the Brooklyn Bridge and the Manhattan skyline in the background before walking to The River Cafe. We arrive at the restaurant at five thirty, and my stomach grumbles at the thought of the dinner awaiting us.

I offer to escort Lucy into the restaurant like I did at the courthouse. She blatantly ignores me and follows behind the newlywed couple. This woman. I can't explain it, but with every rebuff she burrows deeper beneath my skin.

I rub my hand across my jaw and lag behind. Not that I'm complaining. The view from the rear is as mesmerizing as the rest of her. As if she senses my perusal, she glares at me over her shoulder.

If she were any other woman, I'd sprinkle on a little charm and have her eating from the palm of my hand. But I doubt that will work with Lucy. She's sharp and shrewd. I can't help but wonder if she's fighting whatever this is brewing between us or she truly has no interest in pursuing it.

The romantic lighting and delicate music from a live string quartet floats through the open air outside of the restaurant. The waiter leads us to a garden area outside where the table sits beside a romantic dance floor strung with tiny, sparkling lights. Once we reach our table, I can't help but feel like the third, well, fourth wheel. Ben and Penelope have eyes only for each other, no matter how hard they try to include us in the conversation. Lucy seems equally uncomfortable. She takes a healthy drink of her wine and avoids my gaze.

I glance around noting how empty the restaurant is and wonder if Ben pulled some strings to ensure we'd be the only guests out here tonight. He's such a romantic, even though he'd never admit it.

After we order, Penelope jumps to her feet and pulls Ben toward the small dance floor. I watch with equal parts horror and amazement because I know Ben has no rhythm whatsoever. Yet I'm stupefied when Ben pulls her into his arms and waltzes her across the floor with ease.

"Well, fuck me."

Lucy chokes on her wine.

I turn in time to see her flushed face disappear behind a large white napkin. She coughs a few times attempting to clear her throat.

"Was it something I said?" I lean a bit closer.

Her green eyes appear over the napkin and narrow as though honing in on my person, ready to deploy a heat-seeking missile. She clears her throat a few more times before setting the napkin aside. Color blooms in her cheeks and I'm left wondering if it's the same color that paints her skin when she climaxes.

A wicked smile curves my lips. Her frown deepens.

I stand and offer my hand. "Let's dance."

"Why?" Skepticism plays across her delicate features.

"Because this is a wedding, and we should be celebrating with our friends." I grab her hand and pull her to her feet.

Lucy fights against my hold for a moment but concedes and follows me to the dance floor. I place my left hand on her hip and take her hand with my right. She's rigid against me and her gaze remains fixed on something in the distance.

"Relax," I murmur, drawing her closer. Her satin gown slides against my suit creating friction and heat. She softens against me a fraction. "I don't bite hard."

She scoffs and tries to pull away. I hold her tight and spin her on the floor.

"Must you make everything a sexual innuendo?"

"I apologize. I wasn't aware I was." Her scent teases me, a sweet touch of coconut and honey. I want to bury myself in her hair and devour her.

We dance in silence for a moment and our surroundings fade into the background.

"We can't do this." Her words are so soft, I barely hear them.

"Do what?"

"This. Whatever this is."

"Dancing?" I can't help but tease. I know exactly what she's talking about, but I want her to work for this. I want to hear the words from her sinful looking mouth.

"Evan," she growls my name and instantly I'm hard. "Don't make me say it."

"Say what?" I layer extra charm into those two syllables.

"I refuse to ruin my friendship with Penelope and Ben over a fling." Her piercing eyes bore into mine. "That's all it would be. A fling. A one-night stand. Nothing more."

The air around us goes still as the music comes to an end. We stand there staring at each other. I want to kiss her and prove her wrong. We could be so much more. Can't she feel it? This chemistry between us?

"So you feel it too?" I grin. "We can make it work." She fits against me perfectly and I refuse to release her.

"No, Evan. We can't." She pulls away and turns her back to me...to us.

Disappointment and I are old friends, but this time it leaves me off-balance and floundering. The loss is poignant and it settles deep in the pit of my stomach with finality. It was over before it ever had a chance to begin. That knowledge hurts more than nearly losing the business I built from scratch.

We return to the table and pretend everything is fine for Penelope and Ben's sake. They don't need to know. But I can't help but wonder what might have been if she'd only have given me a chance.

CHAPTER TWO
CHRISTMAS CATASTROPHE

LUCY

DECEMBER

The brownstone practically vibrates with the volume of the Christmas music inside. I pull my coat tighter around my throat and stare at the front door. I should turn around and go home. No one will notice if I don't show up. I groan and stomp my feet like an indignant toddler.

Holidays are the worst. I avoided them for years with my own family. Work. Overtime. Picking up a shift for a friend who wants to spend time with her family during the holiday. But this year, I have no excuse. The head nurse nearly locked me out of the building when I left last night. She told me to have some fun. Said it wasn't healthy to work all the time and not take a break to recharge.

But I like work. And I really, truly hate holidays. Christmas is the worst of them all. There's nothing holly or jolly about any of it. There hasn't been for years.

I lift my hand to knock and drop it. I cringe knowing the disappointment I'll cause Penelope if I don't make an appearance. This is her first Christmas as a married woman, and she wants me to be a part of it. Damn it. I hope she has my whisky on hand. I'll need it tonight.

"Suck it up, buttercup." I bolster my courage and bang my fist on the door so hard it makes the wreath bounce.

The door swings open. Penelope's glowing expression is the last thing I see before she wraps her arms around me and pulls me into a fierce hug.

"Lucy! I'm so glad you came." She squeezes me tighter. "I know how much you hate the holidays, but it wouldn't be any fun without you." Her words fill me with shame for even considering bailing on her moments before.

She grabs my hand and pulls me into the house. I push the door shut before she peels my coat off and hangs it in the hallway closet.

My gaze drifts over the decorations strewn across every possible surface of the house. Garlands, tinsel, lights of all shapes and sizes, ornaments hanging from the archways and ceiling. As we weave deeper into the house, I notice a decorated tree in each corner. My head hurts, my eyes burn. I've stepped into a Christmas fucking wonderland. Anxiety stalks forward to the front of my mind threatening to consume me. It takes phenomenal restraint to not turn, grab my coat, and bolt out into the cold December night.

"The place looks amazing." I force a smile and focus on my friend instead of the glittering decorations surrounding me. "You really go all out, don't you?"

Penelope shrugs. "Most of this was Ben's idea. I didn't realize he was such a festive person." She giggles as we weave through the guests mingling in clusters throughout the house. I don't recognize anyone, but I take it as a blessing because I feel like I'm crawling out of my skin right now.

"He doesn't seem like the type." I shake my head and return my focus to our conversation.

"No, he doesn't. Does he?" She leads the way into the kitchen where Ben is pouring drinks. The pair of reindeer antlers covered in twinkling lights sprouting from his head distracts from the typical severity of his demeanor. My gaze drops to the Darth-Vader-themed red and black ugly sweater he's sporting.

I'll never be able to look at him the same way again. Who knew he was such a nerd? I chuckle and some of the tension in my mind subsides.

Ben glances up and lifts a tumbler with a good three fingers of whisky. "Hey, Lucy. Thanks for coming."

"Thanks, Ben. Nice rack." I wink and take the glass.

His lips quirk at my comment. Penelope rounds the island and hugs him. Her red and green plaid dress glitters under the light. The pair of them look like they belong on the cover of a *Good Housekeeping* Christmas Special.

A twinge of jealousy ricochets through me. I quickly push it away and take a sip of the whisky. Glenlivet. "Oh, Ben, you're a saint. This is the good shit."

"Only the best for you." He grins revealing dimples, and I can see exactly why Penelope fell in love with him.

"Oh, crap, the pie!" Penelope grabs an oven mitt and rushes to save the dessert.

I smile and sip my whisky.

"Evan is here." Ben's casual remark catches me off guard and I choke on the mouthful of liquor.

After I regain my ability to breathe, I glare at Ben. "Penelope told me he was out of town for Christmas."

Ben shrugs. "Changed his mind, I guess."

My scowl deepens. "Does he know I'm here?"

Before Ben can respond, his gaze flickers to a spot beyond my shoulder. I turn and immediately regret it.

"Hey, Lucy." Evan joins us in the kitchen. His roguish smile and perfectly styled dark blond hair only amplify the playboy vibe he has going on.

I swallow the lump in my throat and force a smile. "Evan."

"Want another one?" Ben gestures to the empty glass in Evan's hand.

"Sure." He hands his glass to Ben, but his gaze remains firmly on me.

My body warms under his scrutiny. Shit. I knew this was a bad idea.

"Excuse me." I turn and weave my way through the guests, searching for quiet. I need space to think. My feet carry me up the stairs and don't stop until after I push open the door leading to the rooftop.

The cold air bites into my skin and I welcome the

abrasive rush. I down the liquor left in the glass clutched in my hand. The overcast night sky hides the moon from view. Streetlights and the bright windows of nearby buildings provide a hazy light illuminating my path. I focus my breathing deep into the pit of my stomach and release slowly, repeating over and over until the impending panic ebbs into some semblance of calm.

I wrap arms around my torso wishing I had grabbed my coat. I can't go back inside. Not yet. But I can't leave yet either. It would break Penelope's heart, even though she understands. A tear breaks the barrier and I angrily swipe it away. *No. Not now.*

My breath catches at the sound of the door opening behind me. If I remain still, maybe I'll blend into the rooftop and disappear.

A cocoon of warmth envelops me as soft fabric slides over my bare arms and drapes across my shoulders. I pull it tight against me and inhale deeply, fighting the pull of gratitude toward my uninvited companion.

"Lucy." His voice melts over me like icing on fresh cinnamon rolls. "We need to talk."

"There's nothing to talk about." I stare into the distance. If I look at him, whatever resolve I have will shatter.

"I haven't seen you since the wedding." He pauses as if searching for the right words. "Do you want me to leave the party?"

I shake my head. "Ben and Penelope are your friends too. I'll leave." As I turn, he steps into my path, and I'm forced to meet his shadowed gaze. "Don't. Please."

"Do I make you uncomfortable?"

I close my eyes. "No."

"Why are you avoiding me?"

When I open my eyes, his expression is vulnerable and hungry. "Because...I don't trust this."

He hooks his finger under my chin and tips my face up. "Trust what? The fact that I want you."

"You may want me right now, but what about later,

when you've moved on?" I drift closer, drawn into his heat.

"Who says I'll move on?" Evan searches my face and I'm laid bare by the intensity in his eyes. "Why won't you give us a chance, Lucy?"

I pull away and rush past him heading for the door. I need to go home. I need space. My heart rate jumps and my breathing quickens as the panic attack looms out of sight. Inside, I make my way down the hall and nearly reach the stairs when his hand snags my arm. He hauls me against him. His broad body presses against my back. His heat sinks into me and calms my racing mind.

"Breathe, baby. Just breathe. It'll be okay. I promise." His arm slides around my waist and rests there, a comforting pressure as he holds me still.

I want to fight against him, but I can't. I don't want to. When he's holding me like this, I can't seem to remember why being with him is a bad idea. Why we can't at least enjoy the moment...even if it doesn't last.

His lips brush my ear. "Say the word and I'll walk away."

My hand covers his. Evan's sharp inhale tells me exactly how much he wants me, if I didn't already know by the press of his hard groin against my ass. How can I deny this handsome, charming, sinful man what we both want? I'd be lying if I said I didn't want him inside me. But sexual chemistry doesn't make a compatible relationship. A harsh lesson I know from personal experience. In this moment, under the haze of lust and desperation, I can't bring myself to care about anything beyond tonight.

"Evan..." My voice falters as his grip tightens. His breath against my skin disintegrates every word from my mind except one. "Please."

As though my words unleashed a torrent, Evan kisses my neck below my jaw. I let my head fall back, giving him full access. My body ignites with each kiss as he trails them along my jaw. When he spins me in his arms and our lips meet, I surrender completely.

I wrap my arms around his neck and pull him closer,

melding our bodies together as I taste him. Whisky and cinnamon mixes with the heat of his mouth and I can't get enough. He's sinful and intoxicating. I run my hands through his hair and he groans against my mouth, rocking his hips against mine.

We stumble back and hit a door. He glances up long enough to open it and we fall through it into the dark bedroom. He pulls me against him and kisses me again.

One night is all I can offer. I'll make it count.

EVAN

DECEMBER

Holy shit, she feels so good. The eager press of her mouth on mine mixed with the sweet tang of whisky on her tongue drives my hunger higher.

Through the dim light filtering in from the street outside, I can make the outline of her features. She's soft and pliant under my hands. The dreams I had of us together are pitiful caricatures compared to the reality.

She rocks against me when I deepen the kiss and grasps the hem of my shirt, pulling it free from my pants. The brush of her fingertips across my bare skin sets me on fire.

"Take it off." Her command interrupts our kiss. Even in the throes of passion, she needs control.

I press a soft kiss to the corner of her mouth. "Ask me nicely."

"Take it off or I'll rip it off." She nips at my lower lip drawing it between her teeth. "Please."

I chuckle. "Are you always so aggressive?"

"Are you always so stubborn?" Her bold gaze locks with mine.

"Only when I want something." My hands skate along her spine until they reach the bottom edge of her shirt and dip beneath it. She gasps when I touch her skin, tracing her waist to the button on her jeans. I unfasten it.

Lucy pulls away enough to slip my shirt over my head and toss it aside. She runs her hands across my bare chest, and I bite back a moan. God, it feels so good.

She steps back and pulls off her own shirt. The red bra makes me smile, but it's what they're holding that captures my undivided attention. Those glorious breasts. My mouth waters. I knew she had curves, but seeing them uninhibited by fabric blows my fucking mind. I grasp her waist and pull her against me, skin to skin. Her heat amplifies my own, and all rational thought flies straight out of my head.

"You look good enough to eat." I rake my teeth across the contour of her shoulder as I slide the strap down. My struggle with the flimsy lingerie takes moments. Finally, I cup her breast in my hand and her nipple pebbles against my thumb.

Lucy moans and digs her nails into my back. "Stop teasing me."

"You want me to stop?" I alternate soft kisses and tender bites along her collar bone and up her neck.

"Damn you, Evan. You know exactly what I want." She practically shakes me in frustration and reaches for my zipper. Within moments, her hand delves past my waistband and her fingers wrap around my cock.

I inhale at the sweet surge of bliss caused by her determined grip. She strokes the length, shifting my clothes enough to have unimpeded access. I groan and lean against the door.

"Later, baby." I rest my hand on hers. She pouts and steps back.

Lucy turns and hooks her thumbs into her jeans, dragging them down over her hips along with her panties. My brain short circuits at the sight of her bare curves. I jerk my pants down and kick them off to the side. In two strides, I have her in my arms, her backside presses against my aching cock.

"You bring protection?" Such a simple question, and yet it devastates me. How could I be so stupid?

"Yes." Reluctantly, I step back and grab my pants. Inside my wallet, I find a condom and hold it up between my fingers.

"Prepared for anything, huh, Boy Scout?" She takes it from me and rips it open the packet with her teeth.

"Eagle. Made it by sixteen." I grin.

She grabs my cock and slides the condom down the length. I've never been more turned on than I am in this moment. Lucy wraps her hand around the back of my neck and pulls me in for an explosive kiss.

In a flurry of limbs, we tumble to the bed. She rolls on top of me and guides me to her entrance. Shit. She's warm and wet, and I'm not as strong as I once thought I was because seeing her like this has my climax on a hair trigger.

The dim lighting shines through the glass, highlighting her auburn curls and the expression of need etched on her gorgeous face. She guides me inside, and I grip her hips tight.

"Holy shit." I pinch my eyes closed in an effort to prolong the rush of pleasure.

She stills and I take a deep breath. When I open my eyes, she's watching me, her lips parted, eyes glazed, skin flushed. Then she moves. The slow rocking has my body spun tight. Her fingernails rake gently across my chest with every movement.

I buck my hips to meet her, and her moans fill the room. "That's it. Come for me, baby."

The room disappears and all I can see is her, riding me toward orgasm. Her breath quickens with her pace. I brush my thumb across her clit, urging her higher. She trembles beneath my touch as her climax takes hold. Her deep breaths and whimpered moans echo in my mind.

I grab her hip and pull her down onto the bed beneath me. Within the space of a breath I'm inside her again, pushing deep, needing more. I pin her hands beneath mine and kiss her. She arches against me, urging me on.

My orgasm overtakes me without warning. It tumbles

through me, melding me to Lucy, driving all thought from my mind. Just me and her. Entangled and spent.

I rest my forehead to hers. "You okay?" My voice is hoarse.

"Yeah." She captures my lips in a slow, drugging kiss.

"Sorry." I shift my weight off her and collapse on the bed beside her.

We lay in silence until she sits up slowly and scoots toward the edge of the bed.

I prop myself up on my elbow. "Where are you going?"

She picks up her discarded clothes and glances at me. "Home."

Pain lances through me at the distance gaping between us after such mind-blowing sex. "Lucy, you don't have to leave. Stay with me."

Without a word, she pulls on her clothes keeping her back to me. I'm on my feet by the time she pulls her shirt over her head. I grab her waist and pull her close.

"What happened?" I'm confused and hurt. Damn it, I want her to talk to me. "Did I do something wrong?"

She cups my face in her hands. "No, Evan. You didn't do anything wrong. I'm sorry. I need to go." When she backs away, the room's temperature drops twenty degrees.

"Don't do this, Lucy," I beg. "Please."

"Good night, Evan. Merry Christmas." She leaves.

Shit, where are my clothes? It takes me a minute to locate them. I'm pulling my shirt on as I chase after her, but I know she's gone before I even reach the ground floor.

The sound of Christmas carols from the living room sets me adrift in a dream. I lean against the front door and curse. What the hell just happened? Part of me wants to chase after her, but I know it will only push her away more.

Never in my life have I ever wanted to prove myself to a woman, until now. After what we shared, how can I let her go?

I escape to the nearest bathroom and splash water on my face. My reflection reveals nothing of the events of the past hour, but I feel her branded on my skin. Her taste, her scent, the sound of her voice.

I should rejoin the party even though I'd rather go home. I bury the stinging pain of rejection and dry my face. When I walk into the kitchen, Ben and Penelope are serving fresh, hot cherry pie to their guests. I offer a smile in response to Ben's curious stare.

"Where's Lucy?" Penelope pins me with an expression of innocent curiosity.

"She didn't feel well, so she went home." The lie satisfies her, but it twists inside my gut. I take the slice of pie she offers and find a seat in the living room.

How the hell can this be both the best and worst Christmas of my life?

CHAPTER THREE
'A' FOR EFFORT, EVAN

LUCY

APRIL (EASTER SUNDAY)

I wash my hands and grab my lunch from my locker. There are six of us working the floor today, and the ER is slow, thank God, so I'm able to take a few minutes to eat the leftovers Mom insisted I take last night.

The breakroom sits behind the main admission desk. My gaze flits to the door linking the two as if waiting for Brenda to burst in at any moment telling me to get on the floor and tend an incoming patient.

I pop the dish in the microwave and press the buttons. As it whirs, I lean against the table and stare at the pasta stain on the wall next to the trashcan. It's Easter Sunday. My whole family will be gathering at Mom's this afternoon to enjoy a home-cooked meal before retreating to the neighborhood park to hide the eggs for my nieces and nephews. A pang of regret pierces my chest, but I shake it off. I'm better off here.

The timer dings and I pull out the hot meal. Just as I settle into my seat and open the lid, Brenda opens the door.

I'm on my feet in an instant, lunch completely forgotten. "What do we have?"

She waves her hand in dismissal. "Calm down. No patients incoming." A grin blossoms on her lips. "But there is someone here to see you."

A growl rips from my throat. I should have known. Evan. It has to be him. Ever since the Christmas party, he's made it a point to pop by the ER periodically while I'm working. Okay, not periodically. He comes every holiday. New Year's Eve he showed up with a smorgasbord of sandwiches and Tastykakes for the entire ER staff. On Valentine's Day, he brought two large trays of chocolate covered strawberries and roses. Saint Patrick's Day he wore a ridiculous green suit and delivered small bags of gold coins and gift certificates to the local pub for a free pint. Even Martin Luther King Day and President's Day he stopped by with an assortment of snacks.

All the women in the building love him, and at this point, probably some of the men too. I mean, who can blame them. He turns on the charm and it's like flipping a light switch in a room full of moths.

I sigh and gaze longingly at my lunch. Damn him.

When I step out into the ER waiting area, I spy Evan surrounded by the whole staff. He glances up and sees me over the small crowd. His smile blinds me. My heart twists with regret, but I shove the uncomfortable emotions away and cross the room.

"Oh, Lucy! Look what Evan brought us." One of my coworkers, Nancy, coos as she holds up a small, colorful Easter basket filled with a chocolate rabbit, marshmallow peeps, and a coffee mug filled with chamomile tea. "Some have coffee, some have Earl Grey. Which one do you want?"

Evan watches me until Dr. Miller asks him a question and his attention shifts. A genuine smile breaks on his lips and my heart flutters. Shit, I always forget how handsome he is. No, I never forget, I merely avoid thinking about him.

Just like I avoid thinking about that night at Penelope and Ben's. I can still hear the faint strains of Christmas music and feel the soft, insistent press of his lips against my skin. *No, stop, no fantasizing about Evan. Ever.*

His gaze locks with mine as though he can read my mind. I hide my face knowing my cheeks are probably six shades of red. Damn him.

Nancy comes up next to me and offers a basket. "Here. You like Earl Grey, right?"

"Yeah." I take the basket and hold it against my chest blocking the open space between myself and Evan. The more I put between us, the safer I feel, even if it is an illusion.

I smile at Nancy and back away from the crowd gathered around Evan. He's watching me, I know he is, but I can't bring myself to meet his gaze. Halfway to the breakroom door, I feel it. The gentle pressure on my shoulder.

"Lucy."

I freeze beneath his touch. It's the first time since that night and I'm not sure if I can hold myself together. With a deep breath, I steel my nerves and turn. His hand falls away.

"What are you doing, Evan?" I hold up the basket and wiggle it.

"You all work so hard on holidays. It's the least I can do to thank you for all the sacrifices you make." He shoves his hands in his pockets and shrugs.

"Bullshit." I narrow my gaze at him. "Are you doing this to get under my skin? Huh? Trying to push my buttons? Make me see what I'm missing? What?" My breathing elevates along with my heart rate. I bristle knowing I can't show weakness, not with him. Not with anyone.

His blue gaze holds steady. "You refused to answer my texts."

"You lied to Penelope to get my number." I glare at him wishing I had laser vision to melt him into a puddle of goo.

"I never lied to get your number. I asked for it. She provided it. Simple." He takes a step closer. "Why are you avoiding me?"

"I'm not avoiding you." I take a step back and hit the door.

"Now *that's* bullshit and we both know it." He's so close. Shit, I can smell the warm spice of his aftershave.

"Why are you doing this?" I'm torn between hitting him and jumping him right here in front of all my coworkers. I ball my hand in a fist and breathe deep.

"I told you. I wanted to do something nice for you and your coworkers. No strings attached." His smile reflects only sincerity when I meet his gaze.

"Fine. You did your good deed for the month. You can leave now." I wince at how bitchy I sound, but I stand firm.

Evan pulls away, and I'm struck by the loss of his proximity. "Happy Easter, Lucy." With those words, he turns and bids everyone goodbye. Cheers and thanks follow him out the door.

I slump against the breakroom door and frown. Why does that man cause such a commotion? Why does he leave me even more confused with every passing encounter? Shit.

Nancy and Brenda appear before me with arched brows and pursed lips. My gaze flickers between them. They have me cornered.

"What in the hell was that?" Brenda folds her arms across her chest and juts her hip out as if to say *try me*.

"What?" I shift the basket in my arms and shrug.

"Don't *what* me, girl. We could smell the sizzle from way over there." Brenda's intuition is on point, but I play it off.

"There's nothing between us. Nothing." I emphasize the last word to end this uncomfortable conversation.

"Do you smell that?" Nancy sniffs.

"Yeah, smells like bullshit." Brenda snort laughs.

"There's a lot of that going around," I mutter under my breath.

"Come on. Seriously. Spill. This man shows up every holiday bearing gifts and you give him the cold shoulder. What's the deal?" Brenda presses. She'd have made a great detective, which is why she's an admirable asset to our team.

"He's a great guy." Nancy chimes in. "You should snatch his ass up! I would if I were single."

"I'm not snatching anyone up." I frown at both of them. "There is nothing between Evan and me. Period. End of discussion."

"If you say so." Nancy shakes her head.

"Girl, you aren't fooling anyone." Brenda's eyes are brimming with sympathy. "But I get it. You need time to figure things out. Don't wait too long. A man that tasty is bound to attract some attention." She pulls me into a hug.

I hug her back. "Can I eat my lunch now?"

She shoves me away playfully. "Go eat in peace. Lord knows we don't get enough of that around here."

With those words, I disappear into the breakroom and reheat my lunch. As I take my first bite, I pull my phone from the pocket of my scrubs and open the screen lock. In messages, I find the unanswered string of messages from an unknown number I know belongs to Evan. After adding his name to the contacts list, I lock the phone.

This still doesn't mean anything. I don't do relationships. It doesn't matter how handsome or charming Evan tries to be, there will never be an *us*.

EVAN

APRIL (EASTER SUNDAY)

Penelope offers me another slice of strawberry shortcake but I hold my hand up. "No, really. I don't think I can eat another bite."

She pouts and places the slice on the plate in front of her husband. Ben glares at me.

What? I mouth the word and shrug before breaking into a smile.

"Dinner was fantastic, Penelope." I turn my attention back to the hostess. "Thanks for the invitation. I probably would have ordered takeout."

"What are you talking about?" She laughs and sits down at the table. "You're an amazing cook."

"Yeah, but I don't like to cook for just me." I take a sip of my water. "Feels like a waste."

Ben stabs the second helping of shortcake with a bit too much force and it nearly slides off the plate.

"Babe, if you can't eat it, then don't." Penelope sighs and shakes her head in loving exasperation. She turns her attention back to me. "I heard you stopped by the hospital today."

"Yeah. I took the ER some Easter baskets as a thank you for all their hard work." I'm careful to avoid mentioning Lucy with Penelope and Ben since they have no idea what happened between us.

"That's so sweet of you. I'm sure they appreciated it." Penelope takes the plate from Ben who is now pushing the cake around in a circle.

"So Lucy told you?" I clear my throat. "About me being at the hospital today?"

"Yeah, she dropped me a text on her way home after her shift." She dips her finger in the strawberry sauce and licks it.

My gaze shifts to Ben, who's scowl deepens as he watches Penelope with a predator's gaze. I pull at my collar. Maybe I should call it a night. Ben looks like he might climb over the table and ravage his wife at any moment.

"Well." I glance at my watch. "Shit. I should get home. I have some things I want to finish up before the meeting tomorrow." I rise from the table and pick up my plate.

"Leave it." Penelope waves her hand. "I'll take care of it. Ben, would you grab Evan's coat from the hall closet?"

"He can get his own damn coat," Ben growls as he stands.

I throw my hands up. "I got it."

Penelope shakes her head. "Thanks again for coming over, Evan." She heads for the kitchen with a tower of plates in her right hand and the remaining cake in her left.

"Could you at least wait to eye fuck your wife until I've left the house?" I stage whisper to Ben whose eyes remain glued to his wife's backside.

"You're a pain in the ass." Ben tears his gaze away and pins me with a deadpan stare.

"I'll find my own way out." I blow Ben a kiss. "Enjoy those muffins."

Ben lunges for me but I duck out of reach.

"See you tomorrow." I call from the hallway.

After I retrieve my coat and exit the brownstone, I inhale deep and let the spring evening sink into my lungs. I've been reminding myself over and over, things could be worse. Mr. Kennedy has called a meeting to discuss the merger at the end of the month. Our business is booming. Life is good. And yet I can't help but shake the disappointment sucking the joy out of it all.

I cross the short distance between the brownstone and my apartment building. After Penelope and Ben shacked up together, I moved into Ben's apartment. My apartment building burned to the ground last May, completely unrelated to the civil unrest sparked across the nation, and I needed a place quick. Ben had an available apartment. Everything works out.

Well, almost everything. I still don't know what I did wrong. I know I'm not crazy, there's some insane chemistry between Lucy and me. But she's determined to keep me at a distance. I've tried reaching out. I've taken treats to the ER so I can catch a glimpse of her. But she pushes me away every time.

Inside the lobby, I wave to the doorman. He returns the wave and I take the elevator up to my empty apartment. Ben left most of his furniture for me to use. I haven't taken the time to add any personal touches to the place. I'm no workaholic, but I'm not an interior designer either. I just make the space work as it is.

I grab a Yuengling from the refrigerator and pop the top. The cold brew soothes my overheated nerves. I'm still agitated by the whole fiasco at the hospital this afternoon. Being near Lucy always sends me into a cyclone of need, and today yielded the same response.

Once I take a tepid shower, I throw on some comfortable sweatpants and collapse on the couch. Netflix has some new shows listed, but I turn on South Park for some background noise and open my laptop.

After thirty minutes, I close the laptop and push it aside. I grab another beer from the fridge and stare at Cartman dancing on the screen. Brainless entertainment, exactly what I need if I can't have what I want.

My phone vibrates on the coffee table. Probably Ben reminding me about something for work in the morning. I snatch it up and glance at the screen.

Thank you. Lucy's name hangs over those two words.

I sit up and set the beer aside. This is the first time she's ever texted me. I mean, I've texted her at least a dozen times, but she's never responded. My heart constricts in my chest as I read the words over and over again. I'm terrified to respond. What if I fuck things up worse?

You're welcome. I send my reply and chew on my fingernail.

My coworkers enjoy the treats you bring. It means a lot to know we're appreciated.

My fingers fly as I type a response. *You have a difficult job. It's the least I can do.* Cartman's incessant rambling whines on in the background as I watch the three dots play across the bottom of the screen.

What are you doing?

The vice around my heart eases. *I was working on spreadsheets, but now I'm watching South Park and drinking beer. You?*

Reading in bed.

The thought of Lucy in bed has me hard and aching. Don't say anything stupid. Don't. Do. It.

What are you reading?

Murder on the Orient Express. Ever read it?

No, but I've seen the movie.

Do not spoil the ending for me or I'll castrate you.

I send the zipped lips emoji and then add, *No spoilers. Promise.*

Good.

I can't help it. I have to know what prompted this change of heart so I type a tentative question and pray she doesn't bolt as soon as she reads it. *Are we friends now?*

Sure. Friends.

With benefits? I can't control myself. She's so easy to antagonize. I see she's still typing so I wait for the message to come through.

Don't push your luck, Evan.

I smile. *Enjoy your book. Night, Lucy.*

Night.

I stare at the conversation on the screen and wonder if hell was now an ice-skating rink. Not that I'm complaining. Not in the slightest.

Chapter Four
Rooftop Revelation

Lucy

May

Joey and I climb the stairs behind Ben. The fire escape trembles under our weight as we wind our way up to the rooftop. We promised to help prepare a special surprise for Penelope, but I immediately regret it considering this isn't how I want to die.

"Ben, are you sure about this?" I grip the railing tighter with my free hand.

"Of course." Ben doesn't even glance over his shoulder at me. His confidence, however, gives me enough of a boost to continue up the rusting stairs.

"You worry too much, Lucy." Joey chuckles behind me.

Once we reach the rooftop, I stop and close my eyes, leaning against the solid gardening shed. My heart is beating too fast. I check my pulse. Shit, calm down. "You two can bring up the rest. I'm not setting foot on that death trap again."

"Let me help you." My eyes fly open. Evan grabs the bag from my hand and smiles. "Glad they let you have the evening off, Lucy."

I clear my throat and push away the flutter in my chest. Nope. Friends. Remember. Just friends. "Yeah, well, Penelope needed some estrogen here to balance out all the testosterone."

He smirks before turning away with the bag in his hand. My gaze rakes over his disheveled golden hair across the aquamarine button-down shirt pulled tight over his broad shoulders and down to his jean-clad backside. *Oh God.* That truly is a homegrown, grade-A American ass right there.

"Just friends," I mutter under my breath. *You could have had more. But you don't do relationships, remember?* I swat the thoughts from my mind and focus on helping Ben set the table while Joey and Evan finish stringing the last of the lights.

Ben glances at his watch. "I'll get Penelope. Pour the wine. I'll be right back." He disappears in the house, leaving the three of us to finish the last-minute preparations.

I fumble with the corkscrew a few times. It slips and slices across my thumb. "Damn it."

"Gimme that." Joey grabs the bottle from my hand and picks up the discarded weapon that gouged my thumb.

"You okay?" Evan comes up beside me and offers a clean paper towel.

"Yeah, it's superficial. No stitches needed." I press the towel to the wound and hiss at the pinch of pressure and pain.

"Let me see." Evan takes my hand.

My body warms at the touch. His familiar scent blankets me and I'm immediately transported to another, much colder night on this rooftop when he came to my rescue.

"I think I can handle it." I scoff, but I don't pull away.

"I know." He peels back the bloody towel and inspects the cut. "But I wanted an excuse to touch you." The whispered words sink beneath my skin into my soul before my brain registers what he said. Gooseflesh forms on my arms. A shiver ripples through me regardless of the mid-seventies temperature.

I pull my hand away and grasp my thumb to maintain pressure. "Evan." It's a warning, not an endearment.

He lifts his hands in supplication and backs away. Before

he turns, he winks.

Speechless, I stare after him as he offers to help Joey with the wine. What is happening? I thought we had an understanding. Irritated, I snatch my purse, pull a bandage from the small kit I carry with me, and wrap it around my thumb.

After I texted him on Easter, we fell into a friendly rhythm. Every now and again he texts an inappropriate meme or makes a teasing comment. The man lives to push boundaries, especially mine, but I stand firm. What happened at Christmas will not happen again. We are friends. That's it. End of story.

When the rooftop door opens, we all rise to our feet, wine glasses in hand. Penelope gazes at us each in turn with tears in her eyes. I'm so proud of her. Her life has changed so much in the last year and a half. As did mine. When Ben kisses her, my heart damn near bursts with the conflicting emotions bubbling to the surface.

"Get a room! Or I'll arrest you for public indecency," Joey calls out.

"Ben, stop hogging your wife. I haven't seen her all week!" I can't help but add my own little jab. As much as I love seeing them happy, I want some time with my friend.

I hug Penelope tight and offer her a glass of wine. She takes a seat between me and Ben, who sits at the head of the table. Joey and Evan sit across from us.

"Listen, I want to apologize." I drop my voice so the boys can't hear us.

"Why?"

"I admit, I wasn't completely sold on your seventh-floor stalker and this whirlwind marriage." I wink. "But when he called me to help get this together for you, I knew you found a good one."

"I can't believe you did this behind my back." Penelope

glances around the rooftop. "This is why he told me he'd take care of the garden this week." She scowls at Ben who's deep in a heated debate with Joey and Evan over what sounds like baseball. "Men."

"I'll toast to that." I lift my glass almost too quickly, sloshing the wine.

Evan laughs and my attention shifts to him without thought. I can't get enough of his smile. Penelope's watching me over the rim of her glass. I want to hide under the table rather than answer the question I can see burning a hole in her mind.

"Lucy, I know for a fact you're not looking at my husband or your brother." She chuckles and leans closer. "Are you checking out Evan?"

I drain the contents of my glass and pour another. "Psh, no." *Please, don't ask. Please.* There's no way I can hide from her scrutiny. I feel the heat in my face. *Fuck.*

Evan looks our way as though sensing our conversation is about him. Penelope smiles and waves. I hide behind my wine glass.

He waves back. His attention lingers on me for a moment and I swear I see the heat flash in his eyes before he returns to his discussion with Ben and Joey.

"You should absolutely ask him out."

"Hell, no. I'm done with men. Besides, I told you before, I'm not a one-man kinda woman." I shift in my seat. Damn her for being so observant.

"C'mon, Lucy. Evan's a great guy. You two would make a cute couple." She nudges me. "It's not like you two haven't talked before."

I choke on the wine and avoid her gaze. *No. Don't go there. Don't tell her.*

"Lucy?"

My face feels like it's on fire.

"Oh my God, spill it." Penelope's mouth gapes in shock.

"Keep your voice down." I kick her under the table when the guys look up at us in unison. They shrug and return to their conversation. Lucy lowers her voice. "We...kinda hooked up already."

"*Lucy!*" She claps her hand over her mouth.

"Everything okay over there?" Evan seems concerned, but I note the smirk pulling at the corners of his mouth.

"All good. Thanks. Carry on," Penelope replies and rounds on me. "When the hell did this happen? Why didn't you tell me?" Hurt and shock reflect in her eyes.

"The Christmas party."

"*My* Christmas party?" She blinks at me as though she's never seen me before.

I nod. "It wasn't a big deal."

"I knew you two would make a cute couple." She grins. "How was it?"

The memories of that night flash as a series of animated snapshots in my mind. Sinful and sexy and so fucking hot. "Amazing."

"Then what's the problem?"

"Me. I'm the problem." I finish my second glass of wine and pour a third.

"Slow down there, lady." She slides the glass from my hand and sets it out of reach. "Let's eat something first, then we can discuss where to go from here."

"Good. I'm starving." I glance at Evan, who's taken an avid interest in our discussion. He strokes his fingers across his jaw. That damnable smirk plays havoc on my hormones.

Ben interrupts the moment with a toast. "To Penelope, who deserved a better first date than texting a perfect stranger while binge watching *Tiger King* during a global pandemic."

"And to Ben, who needed some sunshine in his life." Evan breaks eye contact with me to toss a wink at Penelope.

I shiver at the one he adds in my direction.

Dinner continues without incident. Joey gets a call from the precinct halfway through dessert. After he leaves, Ben turns on some music and leads Penelope to the bare space on the rooftop he converted to a makeshift dance floor.

I stand and gather the dishes together.

Evan covers my hand with his. "Dance with me?"

Temptation steels through me dark and thick dragging me down. My defenses rise up, weapons drawn. "I'll pass." I pull my hand away and finish cleaning up the table.

After two trips to the kitchen, I leave the lovebirds on the rooftop. Evan walks me to the door.

"Goodnight, Lucy." He tucks his hands in his pockets and leans against the doorframe looking like a model from the cover of Today's Man Candy.

"See ya." I walk away before my resolve breaks and I give in to the charm once more.

EVAN

MAY, THE DAY AFTER THE ROOFTOP DINNER

This morning Ben invited me out for a drink after work. I wonder if marriage has affected his brain. In all the years we've been friends, he has never, not one single time, even suggested we stop at the bar for a drink. It's always me who invites him. Not the other way around.

I'm worried.

I slide a folder into the pile designated for Mr. Kennedy when Ben appears in my doorway.

"You ready?"

Shaken, I glare at him. "Who are you and what have you done with Benjamin Statler?"

"Very funny." He smirks before glancing at his watch. "Seriously, wrap it up."

"Fine. Fine." I throw my hands up and organize the last of my desk. Since the merger, my workload has decreased in many areas, but it's already picking up steam thanks to the new management positions Mr. Kennedy assigned to both Ben and me. I grab my coat and turn off the light.

Ben's dancing from one foot to the other, a sure sign of agitation. I want to call him out right here, but I bite back the words. I need a drink first.

We exit the building and walk a few blocks. The bar's sign looms in the distance. When we first moved to Brooklyn, we stumbled into this place on a whim, looking for a quiet place to get a drink that felt a bit more small-town America and less like corporate conglomerate. Of course it became one of our favorite spots, when I could convince Ben to get out of the office at a decent hour, which wasn't often.

Inside, the dim lighting and exposed wood scream old-world charm more than dive bar. The scent of liquor and fried foods lures me deeper into the room. I wave at the bartender and follow Ben to the booth situated against the back wall.

"Penelope, what a pleasant surprise." I corral my shock at seeing her waiting for us and make a mental note to kick Ben later. His impatience now makes perfect sense. He wanted to see his wife, not that I can blame him. She's a beautiful woman who's sweeter than Mom's apple pie. I'd be jealous if I didn't already have my heart set on another bombshell.

"Hi, Evan." She smiles at me before turning to kiss her husband. "Hey, babe."

Ben slides into the booth next to her and across from me. Before I can say anything, the bartender appears with napkins and menus.

"I'll take the usual, Mike." I push the menus toward Ben and Penelope.

"You got it." He waits patiently for Penelope and Ben to order and leaves.

"So, what's the deal?" I shift and lean back against the back of the booth, propping my foot on the seat.

"What deal?" Penelope's feigned confusion makes me laugh. She elbows Ben in the side.

He grumbles incoherently under his breath and rubs the spot where she jabbed him.

Penelope looks heavenward before leaning forward. "Lucy told me what happened at our Christmas party."

Well, shit. This was not the conversation I was expecting. I had hoped they would figure it out sooner rather than later, but I didn't want to be the one who outed our one night of passion. That wouldn't be fair to Lucy.

"Wow." I laugh. "Straight to the point. I like it." My fingers drum on the table as my brain searches for the best way to approach the topic. I didn't want to give too much information. I am a gentleman, after all. "What did she tell you?"

Penelope shifts in her seat, glancing at Ben out of the corner of her eye as if begging him to step in. He remains silent. "She said you two hooked up at the Christmas party. That's it." A blush stains her cheeks. "I didn't pry for details."

"When did she say this?"

"Last night."

Interesting. "That explains a lot." I chuckle. "And you told Ben after we all left, I take it?"

She nods.

The bartender returns with our drink order. Once he retreats, I shift, dropping both my feet to the floor. I take the cold frosted mug in my hand and enjoy the burst of hops on my tongue. Penelope and Ben exchange an uncertain look. I can't blame them. It's not easy nosing around in your friend's sex life.

"So, what's going on with you and Lucy?" Penelope finally asks the million-dollar question.

I take another drink. "Not a damn thing."

Penelope and Ben stare with their mouths gaping.

"What do you mean nothing?" Penelope asks. "There were practically fireworks last night between the two of you. Your chemistry is off the charts."

"Oh, there's something there all right." I know because I feel the surge of electricity every time she's near me. I can't get through an entire day without thinking about her. She's burrowed under my skin.

"But?" Ben says the one word as though he knows the answer already.

I meet his gaze head on and hold it. "She doesn't want a relationship."

Ben nods and leans back.

Penelope groans. "I knew she was stubborn. She admitted as much to me last year when I was trying to figure out what to do with you." She jabs her husband's side again.

He grabs her hand and kisses the tip of her finger before interlacing his fingers with hers.

"You two need a moment alone?" I can't help but tease them. They're so sweet together my teeth hurt.

Penelope waves her free hand. "Oh, stop."

"Look, I get it. You're worried about me and Lucy. But if she doesn't want to pursue this, then I'm not going to force her."

"Is that why you asked for her number and why you've been taking treats to the hospital staff?" Her eyes shine bright. "You've been trying to slowly win her over."

Ben warned me she was a hopeless romantic. Now I finally see it in action. "Yeah. I guess you could say that. Truth is, I wanted an excuse to see her." I take a drink. "Up until a month ago, she wouldn't even return my texts."

"Really?" She frowns. "You asked for her number around Christmas." Realization transforms her whole mood. "Oh, shit. I should have known something went down when you asked for her phone number and she started avoiding us for work."

"If she keeps that schedule up, she'll work herself to death." I turn my attention to Ben. "Sound familiar?"

"I get it. Workaholic and afraid of commitment. Lucy and I are similar. Point taken. What do you want me to say?" Ben scowls before downing half his beer.

"What made Ben get his head out of his ass?" I ask Penelope pointedly ignoring the glowering stare from my best friend.

"Once he realized what he was missing, he wised up." She presses a kiss to Ben's hand before dropping it. Her eyes widen. "I've got it. It's perfect." The little dance she does in her seat causes Ben and I to share a look of concern.

"You want to share this stroke of genius?" I cradle the beer in my hands and focus all my attention on Penelope.

"Ben and I are going home to see his family in a few weeks." She practically pulses with excitement.

"Yeah. You're staying at the cabin, right?" Where the hell is she going with this? How will this help me win Lucy over?

She nods. "Lucy needs a true holiday. That girl hasn't taken a vacation in years, at least that's what she told me. And I know for a fact she's never been outside of the tri-state area. Can she borrow your cabin for the week?"

I start to see her plan forming. "So, you're going to take Lucy with you to Shipshewana, Indiana?" I can't help but laugh. "Has she ever been to a city with a population less than thirty thousand?"

"I doubt it."

"Or slept in a cabin without air conditioning?"

"Probably not."

"I can't see this backfiring." I run my hand through my hair. "Where do I fit into this?"

"All you have to do is show up and be your charming self." Penelope winks.

I stare at Ben who seems as unconvinced as I am that this plan has a snowball's chance in hell of success. "Whatever you say."

"Trust me. There will be fireworks this summer. I guarantee it."

I shake my head and finish my beer before flagging the bartender down for another. It's not that I don't love Penelope and Ben, I do. But I know if they drag the sexy city girl to our backwoods town, there are going to be fireworks, but they won't be the kind ending with me in bed with Lucy. I can guarantee that.

CHAPTER FIVE
A GETAWAY

LUCY

JUNE

The doorbell rings. I peel myself from the sofa and answer the door.

Penelope, looking adorable as ever in a polka dot halter top and cut off jean shorts, stands on my doorstep holding a bag in each hand. "Hey, girl."

"Hey!" I grab a bag and motion for her to come in. I spent most of the morning cleaning the apartment in preparation for girl's night. Hopefully she'll forgive the mile-high laundry basket in the corner and the assorted piles of mail scattered across my kitchen counter.

"Gosh, feels like forever since I've been here!" Penelope sets the bag of food on the table and glances around the apartment. "I hope you didn't waste your day off cleaning on my account."

"I did, actually, but not for you." I laugh. "This place needed a good, thorough scrub. The layer of dust on the entertainment center was an inch thick. No lie."

Penelope shakes her head at my sarcasm. "I'm sure it wasn't that bad. You may be a workaholic, but you're not a slob."

"Well, as long as you ignore the mountain of laundry in the corner, it's all good. I haven't gotten my machine fixed yet, so I've been taking it to Mom's on the weekends."

She laughs and pulls the Chinese takeout containers out of the bag, lining them up on the table. The smell hits me and my mouth waters.

"Oh, damn, girl. You know the way to my heart." I grab two plates and a couple of serving spoons from the drawer.

"Golden Lotus, Yuengling, and John Wick?" She sticks her tongue out.

"Fuck yes." I pile the fried rice and General Tso's chicken on my plate. "Keanu is my kryptonite, honey, you know this." I pop a piece of chicken in my mouth, savoring the flavor with a groan of appreciation.

"I would never know you preferred tall, dark, and mysterious over golden blonde, broad, and charming."

I finish chewing and swallow before fixing her with what I mean to be a piercing stare. "You're never gonna let me live it down, are you?"

Penelope shakes her head as she loads her plate. "Nope." She licks the sauce off her fingers. "I still don't know why you're in denial about the whole thing. Evan's a great guy. You should give him a chance."

"Girl, you know I love you, but if you keep pushing, I'll kick your ass out and watch John kick some ass all by myself." I set my plate on the coffee table and grab two beers from the fridge.

"Fine." She settles on the couch and turns on the TV.

I pop the tops and hand her one. "No more talk of Evan. This is girl's night, remember?"

"Okay. I promise, I won't mention Evan."

"Good." I settle on the couch next to her and exchange my beer for the plate of food. "It's already in the machine, just hit play."

The companionable silence settles around us as we gorge ourselves on Chinese food and beer. I can't remember the last time I enjoyed the company of my friend without the chaos barging in. I worked the last six days, second shift. I could have slept all day, but Penelope suggested a girl's night and damn if she wasn't right. I needed this. The movie sucks us in and it feels so good to veg out for a while. Blissful. When the movie ends, the edges of reality start to fade into view again.

"Thanks for coming over tonight." I turn off the TV. "I didn't realize how much I needed that."

"Of course." Penelope turns to face me with her million-watt smile. "We can always make it a standing date."

Her suggestion is tempting. "Maybe we should."

Concern fills her wide eyes. "I worry about you." She takes my hand. "You've been working nonstop since the pandemic last year. When was the last time you took a break?"

"What are you talking about? I have today off." The forced laugh threatens to choke me. She's right. I have been working nonstop. I'm exhausted.

"That's not what I meant. When was the last time you took a vacation? I mean a real, true blue holiday."

"Who calls it a holiday?" I wrinkle my nose. "It makes me like the idea even less."

Penelope rolls her eyes. "Seriously." Her countenance brightens. "I have an idea. Why don't you use some of the time off I know you've been hoarding and come with us?"

I shift uncomfortably. The idea of going on vacation with Ben and Penelope sounds about as enticing as a root canal. There's no way I want to play the third wheel on their tropical romance adventure. "Thanks, hon, but I'll pass. You don't want me tagging along. I can hear Ben bitching already."

"Please. I promise you'll have your own space. You can hang out and relax. Work on your tan. You won't even have to see us if you don't want to." Penelope's practically on her knees begging. "Please, please. Come on, it'll be fun."

The idea lingers in my mind turning over and over, every revolution makes it seem more enticing. A shiny jewel glinting in the sun. Maybe I do need to get away. I can't remember the last time I left the city. Hell, I haven't been farther than Hoboken since I was a kid. And I do have three weeks of vacation time saved up.

"Okay. I guess I'll go."

Penelope bounces up and down clapping her hands. "Yay! We're going to have so much fun."

Her excitement infects me and I laugh. "So, sunshine.

Where are we going? Key West? The Bahamas? Aruba?"

Her eyes sparkle. "It's a surprise."

I hesitate for a moment, but the thought of getting out of the city, even for a short period of time has me twisted with anticipation. "We're flying, right?"

"Oh yes. I'll call Ben and have him buy the tickets."

"When do we leave?"

"Next week on Thursday." Penelope chews her lip. "Do you think they'll give you time off on such short notice?"

I scoff. "They've been begging me to take leave for months. I think they're sick of me."

"I doubt that." She stands and takes her dishes to the kitchen. "You're a damn good nurse, and they know it. But you're useless if you don't take some time to recharge. It'll be good for you."

"I hope so." I help her clean up the leftovers and send her home to Ben.

Alone in the apartment once more, I pull out my phone and text Doreen, the head of my department. *Need a week off starting next Thursday.*

A few moments later my phone dings. *Finally. It's about time you use all your leave. Go. Have fun. Send the details on Monday for admin.*

I smile. Guess I do need some time to recharge. At least it'll get me out of the city, away from work, and away from Evan.

Evan

June

Murphy's Law seems to be testing my patience today. My flight into Fort Wayne was delayed by three hours. I managed to make it to the rental car stand before the desk closed. Now, stuffed in my tiny, cheap compact car reeking of stale cigarettes, I'm navigating a detour around a closed bridge, which tacks an extra forty-five minutes onto my drive.

If I were a betting man, I wouldn't play the lottery today, that's for damn sure. I crank up the tunes and sip the energy drink I picked up at the gas station to wash down a hot dog and a bag of licorice sticks. I would have much rather been enjoying Mom's pot roast and mashed potatoes. My stomach gives a lurch in protest of the grab-and-go meal I forced down my throat.

It's half-past ten. I've been away for too long. It'll take me a while to readjust to the pitch black of nighttime country roads and spacious cornfields lining the highway. I yawn and glance at the map. Nearly there.

Fifteen minutes later, I pull onto the long driveway leading me home. The gravel road crunches under my tires and I roll down the window, letting the warm summer breeze drift through. I can taste the humidity.

The lights are on when I roll to a stop behind the house. I park beside Dad's pickup and roll the window up before I turn off the ignition.

Mom's out the back door before I'm even out of the car.

"Hey, Mom." I hug her tight. "You didn't have to wait up."

"I haven't seen you in over a year and a half. You think I'd let you come home to a dark house." She shakes her head and tuts her disapproval. "Now, grab your bag and get inside. Did you eat?"

"I grabbed something from the gas station outside Fort Wayne." I grab the bag sitting in the back seat and follow her into the house.

She scoffs. "Then you're probably starving. I'll heat up a plate of leftovers."

"Thanks, Mom." I drop my bag and wrap my arms around her as she works.

She pats my arm. "Your father's in the living room, reading. I'll bring your food in when it's ready."

I pause in the doorway and watch her bustle around the

kitchen. She's wearing the blue patterned apron my sister got her for Christmas a few years ago. A few more silver strands streak her dark blonde hair. My heart pulls. I've been away too long. I would've come home last year, but with the pandemic, travel seemed to be the last thing on anyone's mind.

"Evan?" Dad's voice echoes from the living room.

"Yeah, Dad." I cross to the other side of the house and find Dad lounging in his recliner, his reading glasses perched precariously on his nose and a book in his hands.

"Glad you made it in." He glances up at me over the rim of his glasses.

"Me too." I sit on the couch and pull my shoes off. "Flight almost got pushed until tomorrow." I groan and stretch my legs.

"Mmhmmm." Dad sets his book aside and takes off his glasses. "How's business?"

"It's good." I lean back and relax enjoying the familiarity of being home. "Just merged with another company, so things are different. Good. But different. It's kinda nice not being in charge anymore though."

"I'm sure. That's a lot of stress."

"So's farming, Dad." I chuckle.

He nods. "Ain't that the truth."

"Have you been out to check on the cabins lately?"

"Checked on them a few weeks ago. Everything looks solid. Probably need to be aired out and a good cleaning. No one has used them since last summer."

Mom comes in carrying plate heaped with pot roast and mashed potatoes smothered in thick, savory gravy. The smell sends me straight to heaven. She hands me the plate.

"Thanks, Mom. I've been craving this." I dig in and flashes of my childhood replay with every delightful bite. "So good. Even better than I remember."

Mom beams at the compliment but shakes a finger at me. "Don't talk with your mouth full, Evan."

I nod and swallow. "Yes, ma'am."

She fusses with her apron and returns to the kitchen.

Two seconds later she reappears with a glass of lemonade and sets it on the side table next to me.

"When are the others coming?" Dad asks.

"Thursday." I take a drink. "Unless their flight is delayed too."

"It's been so long since we've seen Ben." Mom always loved Ben. He was practically part of the family since we were inseparable in high school. "I'm so glad he settled down with a nice girl. Penelope, is it?"

"Yeah." I cover my mouth and finish the bite. "She's a sweetheart. You're gonna love her. Country girl. Grew up in Pennsylvania."

"How lovely." She grins. "Didn't you mention a third person?" Mom adds the question almost as an afterthought, but she knows damn well there's a third person and their gender.

"Lucy." I study Mom's expression. I know she's excited at the prospect of me finding someone. I'm the only one of my siblings who isn't married yet, and being the only boy, I know she's anxious for me to find someone who will make me happy.

"That's it. Lucy. She's friends with Penelope, right?"

"Yes." I hold up my fork and shake it in her direction. "Don't play matchmaker, Mom. I'm warning you. Lucy and I are friends. Nothing more."

I have to warn her. I know full well Ben and Penelope are playing with fire setting this whole vacation up. They're trying to help. But they're still trying to set us up, even if they're pretending they aren't. The last thing I need is my parents jumping into this game too.

"Of course, dear." She shrugs and gives a little sniff as though I've offended her in some way. "I would never do that."

"Mom. The last time I was home you tried to set me up with Mrs. Carlisle's granddaughter who was visiting from Chicago."

"She was a business major who was looking at job

opportunities."

"Mom, she was twenty and hadn't even graduated college yet." I stand up to take my empty plate into the kitchen. Dad's sitting in his chair with a lopsided grin on his face. He knows. "Promise me you both will make her—them—feel welcome."

"Of course, sweetheart." Mom's eyes twinkle at the possibilities. I can see it.

I sigh in defeat. "I'm going to bed. I have three days to get these cabins ready. You able to help, Dad?"

"Yeah, I can do that." Dad slowly rocks to his feet and arches his back when he stands.

"I'll bring fresh linens out and make up the beds," Mom offers.

I kiss her cheek. She takes the plate from my hand.

"Get some rest. I love you."

"Love you too, Mom." I turn to the old man. "Night, Dad."

"Night."

I heft my bag and carry it up the staircase. My room hasn't changed since the day I left for New York twelve years ago. Mom put some fresh towels on the bed, and the scent of lavender and lemon cleaning spray lingers in the air. I chuckle at the posters on the wall. The Matrix and Laura Croft. I shake my head. It's like a time warp.

I stare at the narrow twin bed and sigh. At least it's only for one night. The cabin's beds are bigger and more comfortable. I laugh.

Once Lucy realizes it's my cabin, she's probably going to demand to go to a hotel. Oh, well. If she wants space, I'll let her have it. I have one week to convince her there's more than chemistry between us.

CHAPTER SIX
LIES AND OMISSIONS

LUCY

JUNE

"**Y**ou okay back there?" Penelope asks from the front seat of the rental car.

"I'm still not talking to you." I grumble. "I can't believe you lied to me."

"I didn't lie to you." She turns and tips her sunglasses down so I can see her eyes. "But would you have agreed to come if I told you we were going to Ben's hometown?"

"You mean Bumblefuck, Indiana." I huff and stare out the window at the endless cornfields. It feels surreal seeing wide open space without a building obscuring my view. The whole scene is like something out of a movie. A horror movie.

Ben snorts, trying to hide a laugh, I think. Irritated, I dig my knee into the back of his seat.

"Hey, don't take this out on me." He grumbles something about women under his breath.

Penelope slaps his arm and turns back to me. "Don't put this on me. I thought it would be a good idea for you to get away from the city for a while."

"You wanted me to get away from humanity you mean. Look around, Penelope. The cows outnumber the people. We're now the children of the corn." I slump deeper into the seat and fold my arms across my chest.

"Give it a chance, please. We haven't even gotten to the cabin yet." Penelope's excitement bubbles to the surface.

"Have you been there?"

"No, but Ben showed me pictures. The lake is gorgeous. The cabins are so quaint and homey."

I shake my head. "Why did I let you talk me into this insanity?"

"Oh stop. Come on. Give it a few days. It'll grow on you, I promise."

How can she be so damn optimistic? The last time I took a vacation we ended up at the Jersey Shore for four days of hell. I've never seen this part of the country, and frankly, I have no desire to see it. They're called flyover states for a reason. Which is laughable, since today was the first time I flew anywhere.

When we got to the airport and I saw the destination on my ticket, I nearly strangled Penelope right there in line at JFK's security checkpoint. It was a low blow, making me think I was on my way to some tropical paradise and then dropping me in the middle of a redneck's wet dream. I ignored both her and Ben during the entire flight and most of the car ride. My expectations are shattered and I don't hold much hope of there being anything worth salvaging from this trip. Has it been a week yet? I close my eyes and let the car rock me to sleep.

"Lucy." Penelope's voice shakes me from the halfway haze of restless sleep. "We're here."

I wrench my eyes open in time to see Ben turn down a dirt road leading into a dense grove of trees. After a few minutes, the trees thin and a lake appears. The sun shines on the surface, giving it a mirrorlike glaze. Shades of green and blue mingle with the afternoon sunshine to paint an almost picturesque vista. It looks so peaceful and perfect.

Ben pulls up to a pair of cabins situated beside the lake. I step out of the car and the humidity slams into me. It's sticky and moist and oh, man, I need a shower.

"That's yours." Ben hands me my bag and points to the cabin on the right. "We'll be in here." He shrugs to the cabin on the left.

The cabins are nearly identical in construction. They're

tiny, one-story buildings with wooden paneling and gentle, sloping green rooftops crowned with chimneys jutting up into the overhanging trees. I drag my suitcase to the base of the steps leading to my accommodations.

As I stare at it, I'm overwhelmed with conflicting emotions. Relief, resolution, uncertainty, and of course an irrational fear of dying in a cabin by a lake. Yeah, I've seen too many movies. I shake the overreactive thoughts from my mind and climb the steps. The door opens easily and I'm pleasantly surprised at the sight before me.

The interior looks like something out of a *Hallmark* miniseries or *Country Home* magazine. The main room has a well-worn couch and a chair next to the stone fireplace to the right, and on the other side is the kitchen and a small dining table with four chairs. A bouquet of fresh flowers sits in a dark blue crock in the center of the red gingham-covered table. The scent of lavender and lemon mixes with the distinct earthy scent of wood.

I wander through the doorway in the kitchen area. A small hallway leads to two bedrooms, one on each side, and a bathroom between them. The bedroom closer to the lake is bright with a sunflower comforter and vibrant yellow curtains. The one toward the back has a multicolored, earth-toned quilt and cobalt curtains. I put my suitcase in the sunflower room and kick off my shoes.

Okay, so it's not the Hilton. But it's clean and quiet. Almost too quiet. I can't remember a night where I didn't have the hum of the city to put me to sleep. I guess I'll deal with that later.

Right now I want a shower and a drink. Thankfully, we stopped at the Wal-Mart outside of Fort Wayne and picked up some staples. I fetch the groceries from the trunk of the car and put them in the refrigerator, which to my surprise already has a few unopened items in it. Maybe the last guests forgot them and housekeeping forgot to check the fridge. I shrug and grab an unopened Pepsi. This'll do until the beer is chilled.

The soda tickles my nose, but it quenches the thirst while cooling me off. I head into the bathroom and flip on the light. It's not huge. A single sink, a spacious shower, and a flushing toilet. Thank God. I had a fleeting fear of having to shit in an outhouse, and I was not ready to deal with that. No way in hell.

I set the soda by the sink and turn on the shower. As it warms, I peel off my clothes, cursing the thick humidity clinging to my skin. Once I step under the spray, I moan at the cool caress of the water over my skin. Oh, God, it's orgasmic. I lean my hand against the wall and let the spray rinse the travel grime and disappointment down the drain.

I'm here, so I'll make the best of it. This might not be a five-star hotel on the beach in Key West, but it's my chance to recharge. I don't have to deal with the hospital or patients or my annoying family or even Evan. A twinge of regret pricks my conscience at the thought of Evan.

Am I seriously thinking about him right now? I dip my head under the water and grab the bottle of coconut shampoo on the ledge. As I rinse the suds from my hair, the sound of my phone ringing filters over the noise of the water.

"Shit." I shut the shower off and wrap a towel around myself before running into the kitchen where my phone rings off the counter and hits the floor. I bend down to scoop it up and it stops ringing. "Damn it." I open the lock to see who called and see his name. "Evan?"

"Glad to see you settled in so quickly."

I spin around so fast I nearly lose the grip on the towel completely. It slips from my left hand and dangles precariously in my right. I scramble to clutch it against my soaking wet, naked body.

"Evan! What the fuck are you doing here?" I glare at him and set the phone on the table before rearranging the towel around me. He's leaning against the door smiling. I want to ram that smile down his throat. "Seriously. Why are you here?"

He pushes away from the door and places a key on the

table beside my phone. I could lean into him, he's so close. His warm, cloying scent tempts me to inhale deeply. I steel myself against his magnetism.

"I wanted to make sure you have everything you need."

I scoff. "Isn't that housekeeping's job?"

"There is no housekeeping." He shoves his hands in his pockets. "This is my cabin." He leans close, his gaze hot and full of sinful invitation. "If you need anything, let me know."

I'm definitely going to kill Penelope.

EVAN

JUNE

Lucy's hair is dripping over her shoulders. The little rivulets of water slide over her bare skin and disappear into the towel. I want nothing more than to follow their path with my tongue.

My offer stands. If she needs anything, I'll give it to her without hesitation. The don't-fuck-with-me gleam in her eyes makes me take a step back. I have all week, no reason to rush into anything and upset the hornet's nest.

"Is this really your place?" Lucy grinds the question between her teeth as she speaks.

"Yup. Bought it ten years ago." I point in the direction of the water. "My parents have a farm on the other side of the lake."

Her gaze skims over the room. "They take care of the place while you're in New York?"

"Yeah. I let my sisters use it in the summer. They bring their kids to swim in the lake and go fishing. Bonfires and barbeques." I lift a shoulder like it's no big deal.

Her eyes widen. "You have sisters?"

I chuckle. "Yeah. Three. Two younger, one older. They all live in the area. I'm the only one who ventured farther than the state line." Her jaw hangs open for a moment before it snaps shut. "Does that surprise you?"

"It does."

"Go finish your shower and I'll warm up your supper."

"Wait." She shakes her head. "You brought me dinner?"

"Mom made up some plates for you, Ben, and Penelope." I study her bewildered expression and realize she's cute when she's speechless, but I much prefer her when we're verbally sparing. "She wanted everyone to come for dinner, but I talked her down. Told her you all needed the night to recharge and settle in."

She visibly relaxes.

"Go finish your shower. I'll pop this in the oven."

I grab the bag on the porch. When I return, Lucy's back in the bathroom. I hear the water running, and my imagination kicks into overdrive. Seeing her in a towel left nothing to the imagination. All it did was reawaken all the need I've successfully restrained since the Christmas party.

Once the plate is in the oven, I run out to the car and grab the bottle of Glenlivet I picked up earlier. I was going to put it in the cabin with a note, but I wanted to see her face when she realized the cabin wasn't a rental. It was one hundred percent worth it.

Ten minutes later, I pull the fully warmed lasagna from the oven and cut it to serve on a smaller plate. Lucy appears in the doorway wearing a blue tank top and a pair of jean shorts.

"It smells amazing." She closes her eyes and inhales deeply. "Casserole?"

"Lasagna." I set the plate on the table.

She sits down and glances around as if searching for something. "Got a fork?"

"Oh yeah, that would help, wouldn't it?" I smack myself mentally and retrieve one from the drawer by the sink. She takes it and dives in.

I've never seen a woman eat with gusto the way Lucy does. She enjoys her food, just like a country girl. I smile as I watch her.

After a few bites, she turns and stares. "Aren't you having any?"

"I already ate, but thanks." I point to the chair across from her at the table. "Would you like some company?"

Lucy shrugs her shoulder as she stuffs another forkful of homemade lasagna into her mouth.

I grab a soda from the fridge and join her. We sit in silence until she's practically licking the last of the sauce off the plate. "Is there any more?" She glances hopefully at the stove.

I laugh and get the rest of the dish sitting on the stovetop. "Dig in."

Lucy polishes off the rest of the container in no time and takes a sip of her Pepsi.

"You must have been starving."

"I was." She burps behind her hand. "Excuse me."

"I'll tell Mom you liked it." I grin. "She loves when people enjoy her food."

"Liked it." Lucy shakes her head. "I loved it. It's better than Mario's." She winces. "Don't tell him I said that. He'll stop giving me free garlic knots and a two liter of Coke."

"Your secret is safe with me."

Lucy studies me for a minute. When she draws her lower lip between her teeth, I swear it takes all my effort not to drag her ass to the bedroom. "Do you really have three sisters?"

"Yup."

"Somehow I don't believe you." She narrows her gaze.

"Why do you think I hung out with Ben all the time when we were kids? It wasn't because of his sparkling personality."

She nods with understanding. "You wanted to get away from your sisters."

"Yeah. Don't get me wrong, I love them. But they were freaking tyrants growing up."

Lucy exhales sharply. "I know the feeling."

"Your brothers?" I ask even though I know the answer already. Penelope and Ben warned me all about Lucy's brothers.

"Yeah. I'm the only girl, so they were too protective. Always following me around. I snuck out a lot just to get some time to myself." She twists the napkin in her hand.

"I get it." It's never easy being the only boy, or girl in her case, and then stuck in the middle of the pack. "Well, if you want, I'll make sure my family keeps their nose out of who's staying at the cabin this week. Give you some well-earned time to relax and recharge."

Her eyes glitter when they meet mine and I'm struck by how freaking gorgeous she is. "It's okay. I'd love to meet your family. Especially if your mom keeps feeding me while I'm here."

My gaze rakes over her perfect, voluptuous curves.

"Evan, stop looking at me like that."

I blink feigning innocence. "Like what?"

"You know like what. Friends, remember. We agreed. Friends only." She stands up and carries the plate to the sink.

I grumble under my breath behind her back as she washes the dishes. "Yeah. I remember."

"Anything I should know about the cabin or the area?"

I drag myself to my feet and head for the door. "Nope. Just keep the door locked and the windows closed. There's a small AC unit in the closet of the bedroom if you need it while you sleep."

Her eyes flare with surprise. "Are there a lot of break-ins?"

I laugh. "No. But the bears know how to open the door and the mosquitos will eat you alive if you leave the windows open."

Lucy throws the dish towel at me. "Ha ha. Prank the city girl. Very funny. I wasn't born yesterday, asshole."

"Well, try it and see what happens." I open the door and step out. "Goodnight, Lucy. Text me if you need to be rescued." I pull the door closed on her heated glare and laugh all the way back to the truck. Maybe I should've offered to stay.

No. It will only muddy the waters. Slow and steady. She'll come around.

Chapter Seven
Sleep Is Overrated

Lucy

June

"Oh my God. Shut up!" I pull the pillow over my head but it fails to drown the incessant screeching and croaking of what I can only assume are frogs. It seems to filter through the walls and amplify. Give me screaming ambulances at two a.m. Give me fire engines blaring. Hell, I'll take rush hour traffic at this point. Anything to get those green fuckers to shut up!

I climb from the bed and shuffle through my toiletry bag until I find the small pill bottle. "Yes. I knew I packed it." I pop a melatonin and wash it down with some water before climbing back under the blankets.

The air conditioner does little to drown out the cacophony outside, but at least the humidity is manageable now. I settle my head and close my eyes. I've been playing the day over in my mind. The unexpected destination mixed with Evan's dramatic reveal definitely made the trip unforgettable, but I'm not sure that's a positive thing yet.

Dinner was amazing, no denying it. Although the thought of meeting Evan's family makes my stomach twist and revolt, I admit I am a bit curious about his parents and siblings. Three sisters. Wow, I can't even imagine. I thought having four brothers was bad, but living in a houseful of women must have been a challenge. I shake my head. Am I really sympathizing with Evan?

I mean, we're friends now. I don't hate him. I just don't

see anything between us. *Other than hot sex, you mean?* A little annoying voice continues to remind me of what I vowed to forget. But is it possible to forget one to the best sexual encounters I've ever had? Nope.

Rhythmic tapping overhead drowns out the screeching frogs.

"What the hell?" I freeze and listen. *Tap tap tap. Scratch scratch. Tap tap tap.* I sit up and stare at the dark ceiling. The sounds move back and forth over the roof directly over my head. "Fuck this."

I grab my phone off the nightstand and pull up the contact menu.

"Lucy?" Evan's voice is deep and my name sounds rolls off his lips like a moan.

Shit, focus. "Evan, there's something on the roof. Get your ass over here and get rid of it. Whatever the hell it is."

He chuckles, but I can hear his movement on the other end. "Calm down. It's probably nothing."

"I don't give a shit whether it's the fucking wind or a branch tapping on the roof. You need to get your ass over here to make sure it's not a goddamn bear or fucking Bigfoot."

Evan laughs. "Okay, I'll be there in ten minutes."

I clutch the phone in my hand and pull the blankets tighter around me. For ten minutes I'm hyperaware of every single sound. Every scratch, every tap, every croak makes my breath stop. What the hell was I thinking? I'm not a country girl. This isn't normal. Give me the city and all its chaos over this wild uncertainty.

When I hear the soft rumble of an engine followed by a door closing, I finally relax. A beam of light flows over the curtain of my room before disappearing up toward the roof. I hear the scuttle of movement on the roof before complete silence descends.

A few minutes later there's a knock at the door. I crawl from bed and unlock it.

"Evan." Relief floods me and I step aside letting him in.

"What was it?"

He sets the flashlight on the counter and rakes his hand through his messy hair. "Nothing to worry about. Just a 'possum."

"A what?"

"An opossum. North America's only marsupial. Harmless and quite helpful in controlling tick populations." He pauses, waiting for me to understand, but I stare at him blankly since I have no fucking clue what he's saying. "You have no idea what I'm talking about?"

"None whatsoever."

Evan takes a deep breath, and I know he's trying hard not to laugh. I'm trying just as hard not to take his amusement at my ignorance personally.

"Well, there's nothing to worry about. I chased her off." Evan stifles a yawn behind his hand and my gaze shifts down his arm, across the ripped t-shirt, and down the checkered pajama pants. His husky voice cut my perusal short. "You good?"

I snap to attention. "Yeah, fine. Why wouldn't I be? It's just a 'possum, right?"

His smile disarms me. "Right." He turns toward the door.

"Evan."

"Yeah." He stops and glances over his shoulder.

"Can you, uh, would you please stay? I mean in the other room. Not with me." Agitation claws at me. "In case something else happens." I feel stupid even asking, but I know I won't be able to sleep without someone here in the cabin with me.

"If that's what you want." He lifts his hands. "I don't want to impose on your space or make you uncomfortable."

"Knock it off." I gently shove him. "I don't want to be alone right now, okay?"

"Okay." He heads for the blue bedroom at the back of the cabin. Sexual tension clings to his words. "Just yell if you need me."

His door closes, and I slip back into my room and under the covers.

If I weren't so relieved to have someone in this cabin with me, I would have kicked him out for that comment alone. Truth was, I don't need him. I want him. And the realization only solidifies my resolution to keep him as far away from my heart and my bed as possible. I refuse to contemplate what it would mean if I examined this conflict raging inside me too closely.

The frogs have gone blessedly silent, and a rumble of thunder echoes in the distance. We're in for a storm, and I'm glad I asked him to stay even though I know he's more of a threat than any 'possum or a thunderstorm.

EVAN

JUNE

A crack of thunder shakes the cabin, pulling me from a deep sleep. The trees brush against the window, illuminated briefly by a flash of lightning and another boom of thunder. Rain pelts the roof in a furious onslaught. Rivulets of water streak the window as it pours down.

I sit up and run my hand over my face. Maybe I should check on Lucy. If a 'possum scared her, then I can only imagine what this storm might do to her overactive imagination. I scoot to the edge of the bed and search the dark floor for my pajama pants and T-shirt. It's too hot for clothes, but I opted to sleep in my boxers in case another 'possum decided to wreak vengeance for his banished family member.

Thunder rumbles overhead echoing through the building, making the wood beneath my feet vibrate. A flash of light outside gives me enough bearing to find my discarded clothes. I bend to pick them up when another strike hits.

The impact slams me back against the bed and something heavy knocks the breath out of my lungs. I gasp for air, but there's too much pressure. I'm pinned to the bed. Another flash of lightning and I can see the hole in the roof. A large branch from the sycamore tree behind the house juts through it. One of the beams knocked free and missed my head by inches. Rain seeps through the hole and pours steadily into the room, soaking the bed and me.

I can't think about that now. I push against the weight, but it's wedged and I have no leverage to get it off. Shit. I open my mouth to call for help when my door swings open.

"Evan!" Lucy's eyes are huge. "Oh, my God." She rushes to my side. "Can you breathe?"

I nod. "I'm stuck. Get help."

She runs into her room and I hear her voice through the storm. When she reappears in the doorway, I relax even though the beam weighs heavy against my side.

"I called Penelope and Ben." She brushes her hand over my face in the darkness. I know she's looking for injuries, but her touch offers comfort too.

A door slams, and for a moment, I only imagine it's the thunder until Ben and Penelope appear behind her. They're drenched from running through the storm to rescue me.

Ben's oversized lantern shines light through the whole room as he hands it to Penelope. "Hold this up."

"We need to get this off him so I can check for injuries." Lucy motions to the beam pushing against my torso.

In a feat of strength unlike anything I've ever seen, Ben grabs the underside of the beam and lifts it enough to throw it off me and onto the floor. It clatters and slams into the dresser knocking a lamp over with an echoing crash.

"You're like the damn Hulk." I wheeze, staring at my best friend. "Thanks."

"Shhh. No talking until I make sure you don't have any serious injuries." Lucy pins me with a stern look. "Penelope, bring the light over, please."

I blink against the bright light shining directly in my eyes. "I'm fine, really." I struggle to sit up and my side screams in protest making me wince.

Lucy places a hand on my chest, directly over my heart. "Don't move until I tell you to move."

Chastised, I relax back onto the rain-soaked mattress. "Yes, ma'am."

She purses her lips, but I swear I catch sight of a smile. I lay still as she runs her hands over my head, arms, torso, and then down my legs. She presses and prods, asking me questions as she goes. In any other situation, I'd be turned on by such a thorough physical inspection. But the pain in my side throbs enough to keep my body from betraying any hint of desire.

"I can't see any visible trauma. You may have some contusions on your ribs, maybe a fracture or two, although I can't be sure. Can you breathe okay now?" Lucy's in nurse mode, and damn it's sexy seeing her in her element and wielding such control.

I nod. "Yeah. I told you. I'm fine."

Penelope exhales in relief. The tension in Ben's shoulders relaxes, although his expression never changes from the resting asshole setting he has preprogrammed. Lucy, however, remains skeptical. I can see it reflected in her furrowed brow and pursed lips.

"Uh huh." Lucy turns to the others. "Ben, can you help carry Evan to the other bedroom? Penelope, I'll take the light. Can you grab some towels from the bathroom for me?"

"Sure." Penelope hands her the light and darts from the room. A thud and a few swear words echo the distant rumble of thunder. "I'm okay. Just tripped. Power's still out."

Lucy moves so Ben can stand alongside me.

"Can you walk?" He offers his hand.

"Yeah. I got it." I take it and he pulls me to my feet slowly. He gives me a minute to find my footing before backing up.

"You sure?" Ben falls into step behind me as I make my way toward the other bedroom.

I grip the doorframe as a spasm shoots pain down my left side. "Yeah. Give me a second." Inhale. Exhale. After several deep breaths, the pain ebbs into a stinging ache. I hold my side and hobble the rest of the distance to the bed. Lucy's bed.

Not exactly how I wanted to get into her bed, but hey. I chuckle at the stupidity of my own thoughts and another spasm grips me. I ease down onto the bed and relax. My eyes close tight until the tension subsides again. When I look up, I'm confronted by Lucy's unwavering nurse stare, if that's even a thing.

"Do you need anything else?" Penelope bursts into the room with an armful of towels.

Lucy takes them. "No, I can handle it from here." She smiles at her friend and then at Ben. "Thanks for coming to the rescue."

"What about the mess in the other room?" Ben nods toward the bedroom where they rescued me.

"Not much we can do about it until morning after the storm passes." I shrug and the movement shoots pain down my side. "Get some sleep, we'll worry about it in the morning."

"Call if you need anything." Penelope lingers for a moment before Ben takes her hand and tugs her from the room. As soon as the door closes, Lucy grabs a towel and lays it beneath my head. "Don't move. I'm serious." She slips out of the bedroom.

When she returns, she has a bottle of water and some brown pills.

"I hope that's the good shit." It's a weak joke, I know it.

"If by good shit, you mean, ibuprofen, then yes." She puts the pills and bottle in my outstretched hands.

I pop the pills and wash them down before resting back against the towel-covered pillow once more. "Thanks."

Her soft smile is barely distinguishable in the dark. The hum of the air conditioner fills the room.

"Power's back on." I pat the bed next to me. "Lay down. I promise I won't seduce you."

"With those bruised ribs, I wouldn't even try it." Lucy

rounds the bed and lays down beside me. She pulls the blankets up over us both and turns over onto her side facing the window. "Goodnight, Evan."

A foot of empty bed lay between us, and yet it still feels like a canyon. I inhale deeply, careful not to strain my side. "Goodnight, Lucy."

Chapter Eight
The Lumberjack

Lucy

June

With the 'possum encounter and then the storm, I can safely say last night was the worst night of sleep I've had in a long time. And that's saying something because after the pandemic, I was running on fumes and couldn't fall into a restful sleep after a twelve-hour shift. Nothing about this vacation was even remotely relaxing so far.

Waking up next to Evan leaves me off-kilter. It doesn't feel wrong, but it certainly is strange. I sneak out of the bedroom just after dawn. He needs rest. I make a mental note to check his injury when he wakes up.

Twenty minutes later, I sip my fresh, hot coffee and step out onto the front porch. The cabin sits on the south side of the lake facing north, giving me the perfect spread of the sun's journey across the sky. I settle into the wooden glider on the porch and give it a little push.

Sunlight stretches across the lake surface, leaving glitter in its wake. Between the cabins, a dock extends into the lake. Two boats bob in the water where they're tethered alongside it. I'm stunned by the absence of sound. The frogs who made such a protest the night before are now blissfully silent. A gentle breeze skims across the lake. The heat hasn't made its appearance yet, and I'm grateful as I nestle deep in my Yankees sweatshirt and sip my coffee.

"Morning!" Penelope waves as she crosses the distance between cabins. She takes the seat beside me and cradles her coffee mug in her hands. "You're up early."

"You know sleep and I aren't on speaking terms." I shake my head. "Plus, this place might as well be another planet. 'Possums and storms and frogs screaming."

Penelope frowns. "I'm sorry. I was so excited at the idea of you coming with us, I never considered it would be too much of a change and you wouldn't be able to relax." Her expression pierces me with guilt.

"It's okay. I bet the sound of the ocean and screaming seagulls would be just as annoying to someone who can sleep with sirens and traffic shaking the house."

She brightens. "You deserve a change of scenery."

"It is lovely. I'll give you that." I take a drink. "Thanks for looking out for me."

"Of course." She takes my hand and squeezes it.

"You still owe me a trip to the beach with endless margaritas."

Penelope laughs. "I promise. Anywhere you want."

"Now, do you want to explain why you didn't tell me this was Evan's cabin?"

Penelope's cheeks bloom with color, and she hides behind her coffee mug. "You never would've come if you knew Evan was going to be here."

"Oh, so you knew Evan would be here?"

"Well." She stutters and studies the design on her coffee mug. "Yes."

"Penelope." I stare until her wide, innocent eyes reluctantly meet mine. "Please tell me you didn't do this on purpose as an attempt to set me up with Evan."

Her indignant huff is almost comical. "I would never do that to you."

"Seriously?" I scoff. "Ever since I told you we hooked up at your Christmas party, you've been acting weird. I should have known when you invited me on this little R-and-R trip you had something up your sleeve."

"I'm sorry, Lucy. Really. I mean, yes, when you told me you hooked up with Evan, I was ecstatic. You two make such a cute couple." She pouts. "It seemed like the perfect solution for everyone. My best friend and Ben's best friend. It's serendipity!" Her eyes shine with the eternal sunshine-infused optimism I envy and loathe in equal parts.

"First of all, you need to stop watching rom-coms. Seriously, they're messing with your brain. And second, you know I'm not looking for a relationship. I don't need one. I don't want one." I pause for emphasis. "And three, the Christmas party was a mistake. I shouldn't have slept with Evan. I fucked up. End of story."

Penelope cocks her head and wrinkles her nose. The resemblance to a confused puppy is uncanny.

"Evan and I have reached an understanding. We're friends. That's it. So any dreams you have of us getting hitched and making babies is going to remain firmly in the realm of fantasy."

After a few moments of blank stare, Penelope smiles and raises her hands. "Okay. Fine. If you two are only friends, then I'll take it." She sips her coffee. "I'm glad you both are being mature about the whole thing."

I blink. Wow. Okay. I wasn't expecting her to concede so quickly. "You'll let it go?"

"Water under the bridge." She grins. "Want to help me make breakfast?"

Somehow the words of Admiral Akbar filter through my subconscious. *It's a trap!* I shove them away and nod when my stomach growls.

"We'll make it at your cabin. Ben's a grump in the morning."

"When isn't he a grump?" As much as I love Ben, he is not a people person.

She laughs. "True. I'll wake him with some coffee. In twenty minutes, he'll be tolerable company."

"I don't know how you deal with it." I tease her.

"Well, I did have practice with you." She sticks her tongue out.

"Smart ass!" I call across the drive as she jogs back to her cabin. Once Penelope disappears inside, I retreat inside to find a shirtless Evan in the kitchen pouring himself a cup of coffee.

He glances up. "Morning." The dark bags under his eyes echo his mood.

"Morning." My gaze skims over his broad, muscular shoulders when he turns. Then I see the bruise darkening beneath his skin under his left arm.

I reach for him without thinking. "You've got some petechial hemorrhaging around the contusion above your sixth rib." My hand slides across his warm skin. "Does it hurt when I do this?" I press around the area.

He hisses in a breath and stiffens. "Yeah, it fucking hurts when you jab your thumb in it."

My fingers press against his ribs as I continue my examination. "Any trouble breathing?"

Evan shakes his head and lifts his arm out of the way, resting his hand on the counter. "No." His hand clenches into a fist.

"Well, I don't think it's broken." I drop my hand. My fingertips graze his hip and I suppress a shiver. "I would recommend getting it checked out and asking for an x-ray."

"Not confident in your abilities?" He shifts to lean against the counter and takes a drink of coffee.

I bristle at his comment. "Look. I'm damn good at my job. But it's smart to have someone come behind and double check. Two sets of eyes are better than one."

Evan nods. "You're right, but it's not gonna happen today. Nearest ER is forty-five minutes away and I can't waste my day sitting on my ass. Someone has to fix this roof."

Stubborn asshole. I cross my arms and glare at him. "As a medical professional, I cannot allow you to climb a ladder, let alone fix a fucking roof, in your condition."

"Someone has to fix it," he growls into his mug.

"There has to be a contractor or a handyman or someone who can come out and take care of it. Because if you hurt yourself trying to fix it, I swear, I'll finish the job and kill you myself."

He holds my gaze for the space of a heartbeat. I want to slap some sense into him, but I know it's hopeless. He is a man after all, and I was raised in a household full of them. Stubborn shits.

A knock heralds Penelope's arrival before the door pops open. Her surprised gaze shifts from me to Evan. "Morning. Lucy and I are going to make breakfast."

Evan steps away from the kitchen counter. "Don't let me get in your way."

"Thanks." Penelope bounds over to the refrigerator and pulls out the eggs and bacon. "Ben will be over in a few minutes."

"I'll wait on the porch for him." Evan smiles at Penelope, but his bright expression darkens the moment his attention shifts to me. He stalks past without a word and closes the door behind him.

I turn open-mouthed to Penelope, but she's busy digging out the iron skillet. What just happened? For once, I'm at a loss for words.

I can't tell if I'm more hurt because Evan ignored me, or he looked like I drowned his favorite puppy in the lake. Guilt floods me. Damn it, what did I do now?

EVAN

JUNE

My side protests when I pull the chainsaw from the shed behind the cabin. The bruised ribs hurt, but not nearly as much as the bullshit I overheard this morning.

I can fake it with the best of them. Smile and nod, add a bit to the conversation and no one will guess I'm beyond my tipping point. Breakfast was delicious, but the actual event was torture. Just like sleeping next to Lucy.

Irritated, I rake my hand through my hair. I'll admit, I

had high hopes for Penelope's plan. But after the first disastrous day, I'm beginning to reconsider. Maybe it's a warning from God telling me to back the fuck up.

After I check the oil and inspect the chainsaw, I fill it with gas. She may have a point about me climbing on the roof, but I'll be damned if she's going to stop me from doing anything at all. I sent a text to Dad asking if he could contact the local Mennonites for some help making the repairs. Hell, they built the damn cabins years ago. Until I hear from Dad, I can at least clean up the debris.

The branch that fell on the roof is too big for the axe. So, I dug out the Husqvarna I got for Christmas when I bought the cabin. I doubt she's been used in years. Hopefully she starts.

"You find it?" Ben rounds the corner of the cabin.

I turn. "Yeah. Let's see if she cooperates."

A few pulls and she roars to life. The vibration sends jolts of pain through my side. I hit the switch and she dies.

"Let me do it." Ben takes the chainsaw.

"If I let you do it, then she wins."

Ben stares at me as though I told him the earth was flat. "If you like hearing the words, I told you so, then go ahead. Be my guest."

Fuck. I know he's right. "Fine. You do it. I'll use the axe. Thank God I'm not left-handed."

"I'll pretend that wasn't a jab at me."

"It's not my fault you're left-handed." I grin. Ever since we were kids, I teased Ben about being left-handed. Not because it was different, but because it made it impossible for us to sit together to do homework. Asshole was always in my space. I guess in hindsight we could have switched sides, but where would the fun be there.

"Whatever you say, sinner." He grins. When he told me everyone was born left-handed and we turned right-handed when we commit our first sin, I knew he was an asshole. But I love him anyway.

"Fuck you." I point to the downed branch. "Get started

on that. I'll start stacking."

"Sounds like a plan." Ben starts the chainsaw and revs it. He's never looked so maniacal.

After an hour, we're both drenched in sweat. We ditch our shirts and stack the last of the wood onto a pile beside the woodshed. It feels damn good. Manual labor. I can't remember the last time I did something other than fuck or hit the gym to break a sweat.

Penelope rounds the corner with two glasses of lemonade. Her sunshine brightens the day. "Hey, boys, figured you could use a refreshing break."

"Thanks." I take the lemonade and down half of it. The sweet-tart beverage sates the thirst I didn't realize I had worked up. Lucy walks around the corner wearing a green tank top and a pair of cut-off shorts. The lemonade turns to sawdust in my mouth, and I'm dying for a taste of her. Shit. I finish the glass and hand it to Penelope.

My skin itches. I can't tell if it's the sweat or the knowledge she's watching me, but I shove it aside. I'm going to cut some firewood for tonight, and then I'm going straight in the lake to cool off.

"Grab some of that dry stuff there." I point at the pile right next to the green wood we just cleaned up.

Ben grabs a log and places it on the cutting block then steps back.

I heft the axe above my head and let it swing. *Smack. Crack.* The log splits in two. Again and again, I swing at every log Ben puts on the block. My side is throbbing. Sweat pours off my face and down my torso. The sun's rays cook me until I'm sure I'm red and flaking. But I keep going until there's a stack of dry wood for tonight's fire pit.

With one last swing, I lodge the axe into the last log. It doesn't split.

Penelope and Lucy's laughter catches my attention. They're sitting on lounge chairs, sipping lemonade and watching us work. Lucy's gaze burns through me hotter than the sun's rays. She sips the cool drink, her tongue toying with the straw. That tears it.

I grab the log and wedge my hands into the gap where it started to split. With a burst of frustrated rage, I pull, demanding it split apart with the sheer brute force of my strength. When it does, Lucy's jaw drops and her sunglasses slide down to tip of her nose.

Good. Glad it got her attention.

"What the fuck was that?"

I turn to Ben who crosses his arms. "Shut up." His skin is so pale I'm damn near blinded at the sight of him shirtless. "You should get out of the sun. You're starting to burn."

"Shit." He glances down. "I need to cool off anyway. Race you."

It takes me a minute for the words to register, but Ben's already halfway to the dock. I charge off after him. Penelope and Lucy watch as we run to the end of the dock and jump into the lake.

The cool water stings my overheated, sweat slickened body. Fuck, it's good. I dive beneath the surface again and pop up. Ben surfaces nearby with his dark hair pasted to across his forehead. I splash him.

"Don't start shit, Evan." He grumbles. "Remember the last time."

"We were drunk as fuck the summer after we graduated high school." I shake the water from my eyes.

"Yeah, and you nearly drowned."

"Only because you held me underwater."

"I told you not to splash me."

The memory flashes in my mind, fresh and clear. "Yeah, but you're just pissed because I humiliated you in front of Billie and her friend, what was it, Morgan?"

"And yet you never learn." Ben's gaze shifts to the shore where Lucy and Penelope wade calf-deep in the water.

"What do you care?" I shrug. "Penelope loves you."

"Yeah, even though I'm not sure why." Ben nods toward Lucy. "What happened with you and Lucy?"

"Nothing." I splash myself to hide the heat creeping into

my face.

"Something happened."

"Oh, and you're the relationship expert now, huh?" I glare at Ben.

"No, I'm observant." He jabs me in the sore rib. "Ever since this happened, you've barely looked at her, let alone said two words."

I groan and rub my aching side. "I overheard Lucy and Penelope this morning."

"So?"

"Lucy said hooking up with me was a mistake." I close my eyes. "She doesn't want a relationship. Hell, she doesn't want me."

"Well, damn."

"Yeah. Maybe this week was a bad idea. I should head back to the house and let you guys have your fun."

"Maybe you two should have some one-on-one time?"

I gawk at him. "Did you not hear me? She doesn't want to spend time with me. I've been firmly placed in the friendzone. She Sir Jorah-ed me."

"You're lucky I've watched enough Game of Thrones to even catch that reference." He cocks his head and glances at the women. "Take her to the Dairy Ripple for ice cream. Show her the town. Just you and her."

"This could blow up in my face, you know?"

Lucy brushes her hair out of her face, those sharp green eyes narrow on mine.

"Yeah, but what have you got to lose?"

"Everything." I grumble before diving beneath the cool water once more.

CHAPTER NINE
PERSONAL TOUR

LUCY

JUNE

Daybreak comes too soon. Even without an unexpected furry visitor or a tree-demolishing thunderstorm, I still slept like shit. When I glance in the bathroom mirror, it shows. The bags under my eyes give me an uncanny resemblance to a raccoon. I do know that animal thanks to a movie I saw as a kid.

I stumble from the bathroom to find Evan lying on the couch with his arm draped across his eyes and legs extended beyond the armrest. He's shirtless with those plaid pajama pants slung low on his hips. I didn't realize how defined he was until I saw him chopping wood. When he pulled the stubborn log apart with his bare hands, hot damn, there went my panties. Then like whipped cream on top of a sundae, he dove into the lake and reemerged glistening like a seductive god.

The rest of the night, I maintained space between us. I couldn't trust myself to be within touching range. But I didn't have to try hard. Evan seemed content to keep a cool distance between us. Even his easy banter seemed stilted when he spoke to me. It hurt. I won't lie. I was starting to enjoy the little teasing, friendly banter.

He offered to stay last night, and after a couple of drinks around the campfire, I took him up on it. Was it because I didn't want to spend the night alone in the cabin afraid something else would go wrong? Or was it because I kind of like having him close?

Evan shifts in his sleep and curls onto his side. I turn away, ignoring the desire to run my fingertips over his bare shoulder and pull the blanket up.

Quietly as possible, I make coffee. As the pot begins to brew, the scent of the dark roast fills the air.

"Morning."

I catch a glimpse of Evan as he pushes up from the couch, stretching his arms above his head and pulling the muscles taunt, and turn away before he catches me staring at him. "Morning. Want some coffee?"

"Please." He pads past me and heads for the bathroom.

Why does he have to look so damn good in the morning? Mussed hair, sleepy grin, and heavy gaze. The man looks like he just came from the best night of sex in his life. A spark of jealousy ignites in the pit of my stomach. Not that he just had sex, but the thought of him being with someone else churns my stomach.

"No, don't you dare start that shit," I grumble to myself and pour the coffee.

When Evan reemerges from the bathroom, I hand him the mug.

He glances in the cup. "Got any cream?"

I grab the creamer from the fridge and pour some in the cup.

"More."

I tip some more in.

"Keep going."

"Tell me when." I pour until he holds up the other hand.

"That's good."

I shake my head. "Would you like a little coffee with your creamer?"

He grins before taking a sip of the brew and sighing with blissful exaggeration. "Let me guess, you take it black?"

"Yeah." I enjoy the bitter bite of the dark roast. Sue me.

"Do you have plans today?"

I should tell him yes, but my mouth doesn't listen to my

brain. "No, why?"

"I have to head into town and pick up some supplies for the contractor who's coming today." His baby blues glint in the morning light. "Want to tag along? I'll give you the grand tour."

"I guess." Why does his simple invitation make me giddy? I kick myself for being so damn weak but shake it off, determined not to put too much thought into it. *You don't want a relationship with him, remember. You're just friends. He's being nice.*

"Good. Get dressed. We'll pick up breakfast in town." He grabs his clothes by the sofa and disappears into the bathroom.

Thirty minutes later I'm ready. I packed shorts and tanks and a bathing suit for this trip. Nothing fancy. Judging by the jeans and t-shirt he's wearing when he comes back in the cabin, this isn't a dress-up-to-go-to-town kind of day. What a relief. I'm not even sure that's a thing, but I mean, I've seen small towns depicted in movies. That's how it works, right?

"Let's move. Truck's running."

I step out onto the porch. Evan leads the way to a dirt-smeared Ford F250 parked next to Ben's rental car.

He opens the door and I climb up into the cab. How old is this thing? I can't remember ever being in a vehicle with a bench seat. Evan hops in behind the wheel and shoves it into gear. With the windows down, I enjoy the morning breeze as we rattle down the dirt road.

The rows of corn and fields of wheat alternate with other green fields. Tall trees rise from ditches dividing the fields. The sun's barely over the treetops when we pull onto the blacktop. Every so often we pass a field with grazing cows or horses.

We ride in silence for ten minutes until a large sign appears over the ridge. Farm Supply and Lumber. He passes by and a moment later, rows of houses spring up. In the center of town, a large building rises high above the rest. The domed roof and symmetrical pattern of the stone building emphasize its importance and age.

"That's the courthouse. Built in 1895."

I brush my hair out of my eyes. "It's gorgeous." Rows of buildings with small shops line the square opposite the courthouse on each side. Most of the windows sit empty and covered in dust. I frown and wonder what it looked like in its heyday.

Evan pulls up to a diner situated at the corner with a perfect view of the courthouse. "Let's grab a bite, then we'll pick up the supplies."

"You're the boss." I follow him to the door, which he opens and allows me to enter first. We grab a booth near the front window and order a simple but hearty meal of eggs, sausage, French toast, and coffee.

I hide my grin behind my mug as he pours a hefty amount of creamer into his coffee. "So, what's the population of this town?"

"Six hundred and fifty-four, last census I believe."

I choke on my coffee, nearly spitting it all over the table. "Get out. I think there's more people on my street than there is in this whole town."

He laughs. "The glaring difference between the big city and small towns. If you head west on 80, you'll find some bigger cities. Nearest Wal-Mart is thirty minutes away though."

"Well, I'll be damned. Evan Waldorf, is that you?"

My head whips around at the feminine, singsong greeting. A gorgeous woman approaches our table. Her blonde hair lies neatly braided over her shoulder and her sparkling blue eyes focus solely on Evan.

"Billie?" Evan stands and hugs the woman. "How are you? It's been a while."

Jealousy twists in my gut at the familiarity of their conversation and her hand resting on his shoulder.

"It has. I'm in town visiting Grandpa. He turns eighty-four next month, can you believe it?" She laughs and finally meets my gaze. "Oh my, I'm so sorry. Where are my manners?" She extends her hand. "I'm Billie Guthrie."

"Lucy Mackewitz." I shake her hand and admire the pretty blonde in a sunflower print dress who obviously has a history with Evan. It takes all my effort not to indulge in petty passive-aggressive behavior, which seems to be my defense of choice.

"Are you two dating?" Billie jumps right in.

"No, just friends." I note the sparkle in her eyes at my reply.

"Lucy's taking a much-needed vacation from the city. She's a nurse in Brooklyn. A damn good one too." Evan praises me, and my face warms.

"Is that so?" Billie's smile brightens as she turns from me to Evan. "How is city life?"

"It's good." Evan takes a step back and shoves his hands in his pockets. "Really good."

"You in town long? We should get together and have a drink, catch up a little bit." She rests her hand on her hip.

"Sure, shoot me a message." Evan steps aside as the waitress appears bearing a tray with our breakfast. "Good seeing you, Billie."

"You too. Enjoy your breakfast." She retreats to the other side of the diner and joins a small cluster of elderly patrons.

I stare at the plate full of steaming deliciousness and my hunger dissipates. After several minutes and a few meager bites, I set my fork down. Shit. There's no way I can compete with that.

"You okay?" Evan jabs his fork in my direction. "Thought you were hungry?"

"I was." I glance out the window at the courthouse.

Evan sighs. "Lucy, come on. You can't bullshit me."

"You and Billie?"

His lips quirk at the corners. "Are you jealous, Lucy?" He cocks his head to the side. "It's not a good color on you."

"Shut up." I throw a napkin at him. "I'm not jealous."

"Whatever you say." He takes another huge bite, stretching the moment tight. "Billie and I had a thing in high school."

A thing. As in they slept together? What little food I have in my gut sours. I don't need these thoughts in my head.

"Hey." Evan reaches across the table and takes my hand. His warmth sinks into my fingertips and he squeezes. "That was twenty years ago. There's nothing there. Trust me."

"I don't care. If you want to meet her for drinks, doesn't matter to me. You do what you want." I pull my hand away and cross my arms.

Hurt flashes in Evan's eyes. We finish breakfast in silence, and I slip outside while he pays at the register.

Why should I care who he dates? He's not mine. I stare at the towering spire on the top of the dome. Maybe this was a mistake, spending time with him. Being friends with Evan is harder than I thought it would be. Is that really all I want from him? Friendship?

Evan steps out of the diner looking like every woman's fantasy. Shit. This week is going to be the biggest challenge of my life.

But why fight it? Why indeed Maybe I should stop acting like I have my shit together and give in to whatever this is between us before he walks away forever.

EVAN

JUNE

Silence fills the truck on the return drive. I glance at Lucy every few seconds out of the corner of my eye. Her profile betrays nothing. She stares straight ahead, her spine stiff, and lips pressed tightly together.

I run my hand through my hair. Damn it. We were finally gaining ground again, but running into Billie wrecked whatever bridge started forming between Lucy and me. She can deny it all she wants. I know what I saw. Jealousy, with teeth bared and claws out, reflected in those gorgeous green eyes.

It stunned me. Billie was absolutely flirting with me. One hundred percent. Her grandfather attends church with my parents. I know she got divorced a few years back. I'm not stupid. An eligible old flame comes back to town touting success and a flush bank account. Yeah, Billie was cute in high school, but she's got nothing on the woman sitting next to me right now.

I drive past the turn off for the cabin.

Lucy's gaze follows the dirt road as we pass by. "Wasn't that our turn?"

"Yeah." I take the road around to the north side of the lake.

"Where are we going?" Her grip tightens on the door as I open up the throttle.

"Where's your sense of adventure?"

"I lost it last year." She turns to face me and pushes the hair away from her face. "Seriously, where are you taking me?"

"I need to drop off this chicken feed at my parents."

Her eyes widen. "Wait. Your parents?"

"What? Can't I bring a nice girl home to meet my mom?" I love teasing her. She makes such a pretty target when she's all fired up.

"Evan. That's not funny." She glares for all the good it does her.

"What? You're not a nice girl?" My gaze rakes down the length of her.

"Don't push it. I'm warning you."

"Come on. You don't want to meet my mom?" I pout. "But you loved her lasagna." Silence meets my words. "You've gotta be hungry. She'll feed you, I promise."

"Evan, you're a dick."

"I mean I have one, but you already know all about that."

She shakes her head and stares out the window at the passing cornfield. I see her smile reflected in the side mirror.

A couple minutes later I pull up to the farmhouse. Lucy hops out before I can open the door. She rounds the front end of the pickup and scans the yard between the barn, the house, and the garage.

"Evan!"

I spin around to find my mother standing on the top step inside the screen door. She pushes it open and waves.

"Come on." I motion for Lucy to follow, hoping she does instead of bolting back to the truck and stealing it.

Once inside the house, I hug Mom. "Hey, Mom. This is Lucy."

Mom pulls Lucy into a tight hug. I want to laugh at the unguarded expression of surprise on the poor girl's face. She's definitely out of her comfort zone, I can tell. I smother the laugh behind my hand.

"Oh, Lucy, it's so good to meet you. Evan's told me so much." Mom pulls away and fluffs her apron. "How's the cabin? Do you need any fresh linens or towels? How about food? Do you have enough to eat? I can make up a couple of plates for you to take back."

Lucy's mouth opens and closes multiple times as my mother rambles. She holds up a hand once the deluge ends. "I'm fine. Mrs. Waldorf. Really. Thank you for the offer."

Mom waves her hand. "Oh, call me Mary, dear."

"Thank you, Mary. The lasagna the other night was delicious." Her gaze shifts toward me and I catch the glare she slips in when my mom turns her back.

"You should stay for lunch." Mom shuffles through the kitchen moving pots and pans around, making room on the countertop. "Evan, fetch your father. He's working on the tractor again."

"Want a tour?" I offer when I head for the door.

Lucy seems torn between staying with Mom or coming with me. After a moment's deliberation, she nods and walks out the open screen door.

"We'll be back, Mom." I call out as the door slams behind me. I tug on Lucy's arm. "Come on. Garage is this way." I point out the barn, the outbuildings, Mom's flower and veggie garden, and the field where the animals are grazing. A chicken darts across our path.

Lucy jumps and puts a hand to her heart. "What the hell?"

"What? Never seen a chicken?"

She slaps my arm. "Of course, I've seen a chicken. Just not a live one. I didn't know they could run so damn fast."

"Well, they are related to dinosaurs. I mean have you seen Jurassic Park?" I imitate a velociraptor.

Lucy bursts with laughter. "Don't ever do that again. You look ridiculous."

"Well, it got you to smile, didn't it?" I sway against her as we walk.

"Have you always been such a weirdo?" She tucks her hair behind her ears.

"Maybe I'm the normal one and everyone else is a weirdo." I arch a brow and tap my chin in thought. "Or maybe we're all weird and there is no normal. Normal is an illusion."

Lucy stops walking. I turn to face her, and she's staring at me like a cat startled from an afternoon nap in the sun. I'm afraid if I reach for her she'll bolt and hide somewhere I'll never find her.

"What?"

"Nothing." She shakes her head. "Just promise me one thing."

"Anything." I hold up the Boy Scout salute.

She pushes my arm down and starts walking again. "No baby pictures. Please. I don't need to see photos of you naked splashing in the lake. Okay?"

"Well, I don't think Mom has any pictures of that." I lean close. Her sweet floral scent teases my nose and drives me crazy. I throw caution aside. "But if you want a live show, I'm more than happy to oblige."

"I've already seen you naked, Evan. I think I'm good for a lifetime."

I grin because I know the truth. I saw the way she

watched me with hungry eyes yesterday while I worked around the cabin. We stop outside the garage, and I place my hands on the wall on either side of her head. Those gorgeous eyes lock onto mine.

"Keep telling yourself that." I wink and back away. "Come on. Let's get Dad and have lunch. Daylight's burning."

My body sizzles with awareness. I'm not sure how much longer I can pretend. This tension is killing me, and she's the best kind of cure.

CHAPTER TEN
PART OF THE FAMILY

LUCY

JUNE

Somehow I'm elbow deep in a bag of flour helping Mary make pies. Evan and his father took the supplies to the cabin and ended up back in town for some forgotten necessities. He promised it would only take thirty minutes. That was an hour ago. Mary invited me to stay with her and tell her all about myself while the boys were gone.

My nose itches from the gentle plume of flour dust lingering in the air. I measure out the last cup and push the bag aside.

"Would you mind stirring the cherries on the stove?" Mary gestures to the pot simmering on the back burner with a wave of her hand. She's kneading the dough before she rolls it out.

"How many pies are you making?" I stir and the scent of honey-sweetened cherries hits me so hard my mouth waters.

"Oh, six ought to do it." She grins. "Evan and his father can finish off a pie each. I make sure there's enough for everyone to get their fill."

Six pies! Holy hell. "Wow. Do you get these cherries locally?"

"There's an orchard a few towns over with the best cherries. I buy all my fruit from them." She lays the dough out and picks up the rolling pin. A grey curl escapes her bun at the effort of preparing the crust.

"Mom! We're here!"

I whip around as a cluster of faces enter from the back porch. Three women and a smattering of kids ranging from toddler to teen spill into the kitchen. It's an invasion!

"Grandma!" The gaggle of children run toward Mary, nearly knocking her off her feet.

"Hello!" Mary kisses each one on the head in between flour-coated hugs. "So glad you could make it."

I go perfectly still. Maybe if they can't see me, they won't know I'm here. I pray I'll blend into the floral wallpaper and vanish. When Evan brought me to his parents, I hadn't realized I would be meeting the entire clan. My heart seizes.

Each of the women takes her time greeting their mother. The last one, with a baby on her hip, turns to me with a grin.

"Hi, you must be Lucy." She offers her free hand.

"I am." I shake her hand, stunned I can even find my voice. "Nice to meet you."

"Likewise. I'm Jenny. This is Carla, and the one yelling at the twins is Denise." Her eyes, the same starlight blue as Evan, sparkle with her smile.

Even though I grew up in a big family, it always made me uncomfortable. To this day, I can't explain why, so I avoid it. This unexpected family introduction sends a shiver of uncertainty pulsing beneath my skin. A prickling anxiety swells. I'm going to kill Evan if he had anything to do with this.

"Get outside, all of you! Run some energy off!" Denise shouts though the screen door as it slams behind the last child. I'm left with Evan's three sisters, his mother, and the pint-sized nephew.

I mumble a greeting to Carla and Denise, who smile warmly.

"Well, Mom, what do you need help with?" Jenny grabs the rolling pin.

"Finish those crusts for me and let's get these pies in the oven. I want to get this meatloaf in by four." She turns to the counter and begins dicing onions.

Without a word, the girls fall into a rhythm. Jenny rolls

the crust, and Denise places them in the pie tin. Carla sits at the end of the table with the little one bouncing on her lap, keeping him occupied.

"You mind ladling the filling for me?" Denise comes beside me with the crust-laden tin.

"I think I can handle that." I carefully scoop the cherry filling and top off the pies one by one.

Within twenty minutes, we have the pies prepared and in the oven. Denise fetches the iced tea from the refrigerator and pours us each a glass.

Mary shuffles at the counter behind us as she finishes placing the meatloaf in the pan and sets it aside. "There. Now we'll put the potatoes on once the meatloaf is in." She takes a seat at the table with the rest of us.

The tea is strong and cold, and it cuts through the heat of the kitchen. A gentle breeze drifts through the screen door carrying the laughter of the children playing outside. The ladies sip quietly while their gazes drift back and forth between each other.

Finally, Jenny turns to me. "Are you enjoying your time away from the city?"

I nod.

"I've never been to New York City, but I imagine it's a whole different world." Jenny grins.

"It is extremely different, that's for sure." I sip my tea, ignoring the increasing pressure building in my chest. Anxiety threatens to choke me.

The sisters exchange nervous looks. Even Mary fidgets with the glass in her hand.

I get to my feet. "Where's the restroom?"

"Down the hall, last door on the left." Denise points to the doorway leading deeper into the house.

"Thanks." I scoot past Carla and the toddler making my way toward the hall.

Once I reach the empty room, the painful constriction in my chest loosens enough for me to regain control of my breathing. I wander down the hall with my hand trailing along the wallpaper, needing something to ground me. Inside the bathroom, I close the door and lock it.

I brace my hands on the sink and inhale deep, then exhale long. I repeat the motion over and over until the tension ebbs from my shoulders. Hunched over the sink, I shake my head before turning on the tap and splashing the cool water on my face.

As I dry off, I stare in the mirror. *Keep it together. Don't panic.* Part of me wants to run back to the cabin and lock myself inside. Another part wants to demand Ben drive me to the airport. But a small, conflicted voice deep inside wants to stay. Damn it, Evan. It's one thing to stop by your parents to drop off supplies and have lunch. It's something completely different to meet the whole flipping family and face the inquisition. I exhale with a groan.

Only they haven't asked me anything invasive or assumed anything, have they? I curse under my breath. Calm down. Deep breaths. They're not monsters and I'm not under attack. Breathe.

A soft knock startles me.

"Lucy? Are you okay in there?" Jenny's voice garbles through the door.

I sigh and open the door.

"Hey. I don't mean to bother you, but you looked a bit off. I wanted to make sure you didn't need anything." Concern fills Jenny's blue eyes.

"Yeah, I mean, no, I'm good." I force a smile. "Thanks for checking."

Jenny studies me closely for a moment, and I'm positive she can see straight through the bullshit. "Listen. You don't have to worry. We promise not to ask you anything about Evan or work or whatever if it makes you feel uncomfortable, okay?"

The gravity pulling me down lightens at her words. I nod.

"No pressure." She smiles. "Dad called. He says they'll be back in thirty minutes. Why don't you finish your tea and relax with us a few minutes?" She turns to head back down the hall.

"Hey, Jenny," I call after her.

She stops and turns. "Yeah, Lucy?"

"Thank you."

"Of course." Jenny walks down the hall.

I follow behind and sit down at the table, which is now bursting with animated discussion about the upcoming Independence Day festival. They carry on and joke about ridiculous things. I sip my tea and listen, grateful I don't have to add anything to the conversation. I enjoy being present.

Jenny catches my eye and winks before pushing a plate of sugar cookies in my direction.

I take one and smile. Something brushes my elbow. I glance around and see a fair-haired toddler staring up at me. His hand outstretched, his eyes focused solely on my cookie. I lift him into my lap and glance at Carla who's grinning. When she nods, I offer him the cookie.

"This is Charlie." Jenny leans close and winks. "You've just made a friend for life."

Cookies in hand, Charlie and I listen as the ladies' chatter, and whatever remains of my anxiety melts into the distance.

EVAN

JUNE

When Dad said my sisters were at the house with Mom and Lucy, I cringed. Taking her on an impromptu visit to my parents had been pushing it, but all three sisters showing up could very well tip the scales. And not in a positive direction.

I love my sisters, but they are the nosiest people on the planet. When I lived at home, I got no peace. None. They constantly badgered me about everything, and when I did show an interest in a girl, they always ruined whatever minute chance I had.

Dad and I pull into the driveway and park the truck under the old elm tree. My sisters' kids materialize from behind trees, running full tilt toward us. I brace myself for impact and I'm not disappointed. Teddy, my fifteen-year-old nephew and the oldest of all the grandchildren, hangs back watching the younger kids clamor for attention.

Kate tries to climb onto my back when I bend down to hug Nathan. "Okay, you two monkeys." I heft Kate onto my back, and she wraps her arms around my throat. I grab Nathan and pick him up. They're tiny, scrappy eight-year-old twins. Kate looks exactly like her mother, Denise.

I swing them both around for a few minutes until I hear Denise calling from the kitchen.

"Hey, Teddy." I nod to the older boy and offer a fist bump, which he takes.

"Hey, Uncle Evan." His phone dings, and he turns away to answer it.

Since when did the kid grow up? I swear he's two feet taller than he was the last time I saw him. Give him another six inches and we'll be eye level. Damn, that's terrifying.

I give Danielle and Toby a hug and together we set off toward the house.

I brace myself for the fallout when I enter the chaos of the kitchen. Kids running in and out of the room asking for iced tea. Mom pulling pies from the oven. Jenny and Carla doling out beverages and cookies. Where's Lucy?

She's sitting at the kitchen table with little Charlie on her lap watching the whirlwind around her with wide eyes and a smile on her lips. My heart does this weird little somersault in my chest. Then she sees me.

I wave.

She waves back.

I point toward the door. Lucy doesn't hesitate. She stands up and weaves through the people.

"There's my little buddy." My dad slips in behind me and reaches for Charlie as Lucy approaches us. "Come and sit with Grandpa."

Charlie practically launches himself into my dad's arms.

I grab Lucy's hand and pull her out the door. "Come on. Let's go for a ride."

"Where the hell are you taking me now?" Lucy holds tight as we weave through the trees and past the garden. On the other side of the garage, I open the small storage shed where Dad stores the four-wheeler.

"Wait here." I hop on the ATV and start it. She purrs beneath me as I put her in gear and inch forward. Lucy steps out of the way. "Hop on." I pat the seat behind me.

She eyes me suspiciously and folds her arms across her chest.

"I promise I'll behave." I wink and scoot forward a bit more to give her plenty of room.

Lucy rolls her eyes. "Fine, but if you try anything, I swear." She shakes her fist at me before climbing up onto the four-wheeler and settling into the seat.

"Put your arms around me." I glance over my shoulder. She's put a good four inches of air between us.

"What?"

"Put your arms around me, so you don't fall off."

She sighs and slides forward, pressing her front to my back. The warmth sinks into my soul. Every curve molds against me and my cock hardens instantly. Fuck, she feels so good. Her hands lock around my stomach. It takes inhuman strength I didn't know I possessed not to slide her hand down and show her exactly what she does to me. I wince when she presses against my sore side.

"Sorry." She eases the tension.

"Hold on tight." I throw the ATV into gear and hit the throttle. We glide easily out of the yard and onto the dirt road, weaving through the cornfields.

The evening breeze is the only thing soothing the heat building between us. I steer us toward the lake. Dad needs the truck, so I opted for the four-wheeler as our mode of transportation back to the cabin. I shouldn't have left without telling everyone goodbye, but I know my family. That would be an hour-long ordeal, and truthfully, I wanted Lucy all to myself for the rest of the evening. Cherry pie be damned.

We cross the field and slip into the woods near the north end of the lake. A winding trail leads along the shore, and we follow it for a while. The cool shade of the trees makes her huddle closer to me despite the humidity. I feel her body shift as she looks around. Finally, she leans her head against my shoulder and relaxes her grip so her arms encircle my hips.

In the distance, I see a few deer spook from their grazing spot. They bound through the woods. I motion to them and Lucy leans forward.

"They're beautiful," she says over the rumble of the engine.

Once the deer disappear, I push forward. We're close to the cabin, but I'm not nearly ready for this moment to end. Having her this close is intoxicating and it only reinforces my determination.

We creep through the forest, catching glimpses of the lake through the trees, until we break through the tree line down from the cabin sites. They come into view and part of my heart aches knowing soon she'll pull away from me again.

The ATV rolls to a stop next to Ben's rental car, and I kill the ignition switch. Lucy's hands linger on my hips for a moment, her head unmoving against my shoulder. I run my fingers across hers.

"You're back!" Penelope bounds around the corner.

Lucy pulls her hands away and shifts to get off the four-wheeler. Disappointment grips me at the loss of her touch. She lands on the ground and wobbles for a moment.

"When you ride with me, I'll leave your knees weak." It's corny as fuck, but I can't seem to form any rational thought, so I run with it.

Instead of a smart comment, Lucy shakes her head and walks toward Penelope.

"I was wondering when you'd be back. Ben's making a fire." She links her arm though Lucy's.

Lucy glances back at me before following her friend's

lead. If I didn't know any better, I'd think she wanted to say something. Probably a snarky comment or delayed burn. Still, I can hope for something more substantial, right?

I pocket the key and find Ben near the fire pit. "You need any help?"

Ben sits back on his heels and growls at me. His hair stands on end like he's been electrocuted because he's run his hand through it so many times out of frustration.

"I'll take that as a yes."

Once I get the fire started, with Ben's help, I head into the cabin and start on dinner. Burgers and dogs sound pretty good. I grab everything I need and carry it out to the small table near the pit. The small grate over the fire is perfect for grilling.

The girls reappear from Ben's cabin as I put the food on the grate. Lucy hands me a beer and settles into the chair beside Penelope.

As she tells Penelope about her afternoon with my family, I play chef. I wonder for a moment if she's really talking about my family since most of her comments are positive. I don't say anything. Instead, I listen, and what I hear gives me hope there could be something more between us.

Maybe it's time I turned up the heat.

Chapter Eleven
Stargazing

Lucy

June

Long after the sun has set and at least a six pack in, I'm able to relax in my chair next to the fire pit. The clear, star-spattered sky stretches above us and the moon peeks over the trees on the other side of the lake. The frogs croak in the distance, adding background noise to our little gathering. It's like I'm stuck in a painting hanging in a museum somewhere, and surprisingly, I'm not freaking out.

Ben and Penelope wave as they stumble arm in arm toward their cabin. Twenty bucks says those two are about to get busy. I push the thought from my mind. I'm happy for them. Even after a year together, they're still smitten with each other. It's disgustingly domestic.

I nurse the half-empty beer in my hand and stare into the flames.

"Hey, I'm sorry about throwing you to the wolves today." Evan's apology pulls me from my daze.

I shrug and smile. "I survived just fine."

"I know." Evan leans closer. Our chairs are already only a foot apart, but the movement brings his attention solely on me. "Jenny texted me. Chewed my ass for dropping you in the middle of all of that without warning."

My chest constricts at the touching gesture. "You've got a great family." I want to scream, but I also just want the conversation to die. So I keep my responses simple in an effort not to explode.

"You've got a big family too, don't you?" Evan takes a drink and leans back.

"Yeah." *Please, don't do this, Evan. Don't work so hard to climb these defenses I've spent years building.* The sounds of nature fill the void between us.

Evan sets his beer aside, gets to his feet, and offers me his hand. "Come on."

Reluctance pulls me deeper into my seat, but I can't ignore him. I slide my hand in his, and he pulls me up effortlessly. I wobble as I find my footing. The alcohol hits me with every step, and I lean into him as he guides me toward the dock in the darkness. The moonlight guides our way until we're standing at the end of the dock.

"Look up." Evan points toward the distance. "Do you see that flashing light in the sky?"

I follow the direction and frown. "No."

Evan steps behind me and points, laying my hand over his. His heat sinks into me and I'm tempted to lean against him completely. My gaze searches until I see the distant light flickering red and green and white.

"I see it." Surprise and wonder fill me. "What is it? A UFO?" I turn my head enough to study his profile. He's so close, even in the moonlight I can see the tiny white scar along the side of his cheek beneath the stubble he forgot to shave this morning. No expensive colognes or aftershaves tickle my nose, instead I'm left breathing in the scent of him and a hint of woodsmoke.

He chuckles, bringing me back to the light. "No, it's a star. At certain times, when it's at just the right height in the sky, it flashes what looks like different colors. Crazy, huh?"

"Yeah, crazy." I swallow and glance back at the star. "Where did you learn this?"

"Boy Scouts. Astronomy merit badge. Kind of got me hooked on space." He drops his hand but doesn't pull away.

I don't move when his hand comes to rest on the dip of my lumbar spine. "It must be hard to stargaze in the city."

"It's almost impossible. Too much light pollution." He

points in another direction. "Right there is Taurus, the bull, and then Orion here." As his finger moves, I follow along trying to see the constellations as he points them out. After a few minutes, I start to recognize the patterns, and it's beautiful, not to mention serene.

"I never realized how much fun stargazing could be." I lean deeper into his touch when he turns to show me Ursa Major.

"It was always my favorite part of camping as a Scout." He inhales deeply. "Too bad we don't have a telescope. I could show you the seas on the moon." He points to the bright star to the left of the moon. "And Venus."

"Wait, that's not a star?" I gape at the brightest object aside from the moon.

"No. In fact, you can see Jupiter, Mercury, Mars, Saturn, and Venus without a telescope." He points to a red star. "Like there, that's Mars."

"Get out of here." I stare in awe at the sky. Yeah, I learned about the planets and the solar system in school, but I never studied them in depth. I stare into the heavens in complete awe. "That's amazing. It's beautiful."

"Just like you."

I go still. His confession hangs between us, and I'm afraid if I breathe or speak the moment will implode in spectacular fashion. His hand slides to my hip and he pulls me against him.

"Evan," I whisper. "Please, don't."

"Don't what." His breath caresses my neck. "Don't tell you how beautiful you are?" He chuckles. "You're fucking stunning, and I don't care if you don't want to hear it, it's true."

"We're..."

"Just friends, I know." He sighs but doesn't release me. "If that's all you want from me, I'll respect it."

Is that what I want? Truly, deep in the darkest corner of my soul, I know I want more. I want someone I can trust, someone who respects me, someone who understands all of my inadequacies and insecurities. I want someone who's willing to fight for me and beside me. I know friendship will never be enough to satisfy me completely.

Once, I thought I'd found someone who fit those requirements, but he fucked it all up without a moment's regret. After him, I never allowed anyone to get close enough to see if they can fill the nearly impossible requirements I demand. I push them away and shut them out, like I've done with Evan since the first day we met, because I can't endure such pain again. I won't.

"Lucy, I want you to know whatever you decide, I'll always be here for you." Evan steps away, and a chill sinks into my bones at the loss of his touch.

I wrap my arms around myself and shiver. "I think I'm going to call it a night."

Evan shoves his hands in his pockets and nods. As we make our way back to the fire, I grow irritated by the distance and silence creating the unbearable tension between us.

"I'll stay out here and make sure the fire is out." Evan stops next to the fire and picks up a stick to prod at the dying coals.

I pause on the steps of the cabin. "You'll stay though, right?"

"If you want me to, yes."

"Thank you, Evan." I head into the cabin and straight for the shower.

Twenty minutes later, I'm showered and tucked into bed. I stare at the moon through the curtain as it rises high into the sky. Exhaustion pulls at me, but my mind is racing. Why am I fighting this so hard? Why do I push him away? I punch the pillow repeatedly and settle my head once more.

An hour later, the front door closes. I listen as he crosses to the bathroom and turns on the shower. I'm so pissed at my insomnia, at my hormones, at my own fucking mind for turning on me.

What do I want? The question repeats in my mind over and over. I kick off the blankets and stare at the ceiling.

When the bathroom door opens, I don't even try to stop myself.

"Evan." His name echoes in the quiet room, and I squeeze my eyes shut and curse myself.

My door opens. "Did you say something?"

I can't see his face, but his shadowed figure hovers in the doorway.

"I did." I move toward the edge of the bed, making room. "You can sleep in here. The couch can't be comfortable."

"It's not." He pauses. "Are you sure?"

"Are you going to try to take advantage of me?" I tease.

"I would never." He comes inside the room and closes the door.

My pulse quickens when he climbs onto the bed and settles beside me. There's a good two feet of space between us and I can still feel the heat coming off his skin in waves. God, he smells fucking amazing too. I turn onto my side facing away from him. I can't trust myself not to reach for him, not to nestle closer to him and bury my face against his body.

When his hand comes to rest on my side, I stiffen. He pulls away.

"Sorry."

"Don't be." I shift restlessly. "It's just...I can't remember the last time I slept with anyone." I immediately regret my words. Shit. "*Sleep* sleep. Not sex. I'll shut up now."

Evan chuckles. "I knew what you meant. I'm used to having the bed to myself too."

After fifteen minutes of tossing and rolling, I'm about to scream into the heavens. Fucking insomnia.

Evan reaches out and pulls me against him. Two spoons nestled perfectly together in a dark, soft drawer. I relax after a few moments even with his hand draped across my stomach and his obvious arousal pressed against my ass. I nestle closer to him.

"Are you trying to take advantage of me?" Evan's sleepy

voice tickles my ear.

"No." I smile. "Just testing you."

"How rude." He bucks his hips against me. "Don't start something. Go to sleep."

"Goodnight, Evan."

"Night, Lucy."

Wrapped in his warm embrace and lulled by his sleepy voice, I close my eyes, determined to ignore the need coursing through me, and try to sleep.

EVAN

JUNE

What the fuck was I thinking? I barely slept at all last night with Lucy plastered against me. Now I'm lying on my back with Lucy tucked against my side, her leg draped over mine, her hand lying over my heart.

She's snoring and has been snoring for the last hour. All night, as I drifted in and out of consciousness, I remained acutely aware of the woman beside me. Part of it because I'm used to having the bed to myself, but this time I'm pretty sure it's because I had to continually talk myself down from kissing her awake and laying claim to the woman who has stolen the last of my sanity.

The pale blue of dawn filters through the curtains. How I made it until morning, I'll never know. I glance down at the auburn-haired temptation lying beside me. Shit. I need to get the other bedroom fixed and the bed replaced.

Lucy shifts against me and moans.

Son. Of. A. Bitch. Think about doing taxes, going for a prostate exam, anything to distract me from the wicked thoughts teasing me with memories of the Christmas party. I take several deep breaths.

Her fingers curl against my skin, raking her nails over my

heart. I close my eyes and start counting backwards from one hundred.

The bed dips as she pulls away. Disappointment grabs me the moment she slips out of reach. I open my eyes to find her staring at me in hazy confusion.

"Sorry." She brushes her hair back from her face. Her rosy cheeks and sleepy pout warm my soul.

"It's okay. My virtue is still intact."

Lucy grabs the pillow and whacks me with it.

I snatch it from her hands and toss it away. She stares open mouthed as her weapon is launched out of reach.

"Rude." She shoves my shoulder.

"Rude?" I snatch her by the wrist and pull her down on top of me. "You assaulted me with a pillow."

She struggles against me, and I immediately regret starting this because my cock is rock hard and straining against my pajama bottoms. It takes her half a second to realize her mistake when it rubs against her thigh. Her gaze drops to my mouth before locking with mine.

"Evan." Her body sinks lower until she's flush against me, my arms around her waist, her lips dangerously close to mine.

BANG. BANG. BANG. Three loud knocks echo through the cabin.

Startled, Lucy climbs off me and turns away.

I jump to my feet and run my hand over my face as I stalk toward the front door. There's nothing to do for the tent protruding in the front of my pants. I hide behind the door when I crack it open.

"What?" I snap.

Ben arches a brow. "Rough night?"

"Fuck you. What the hell are you doing here?" I glance at the absence of sun on the horizon. "The sun isn't even up yet."

"You're the one who wanted to go fishing at dawn, remember?" Ben pushes open the door and lets himself in. He glances at my obvious state of discomfort.

Well, there's no hiding it now. I put my hands on my hips and stare at him with a frown.

There aren't many times I can say I've seen Ben smile. I mean a real, true, honest-to-God grin. But there it is, emphasized by two dimples I don't remember him having before.

"I'm so glad you're amused." I cross my arms, which only seems to highlight my problem.

"Did I interrupt?" Ben fails to bite back the smile.

"I'm not even going to dignify that with an answer." I stalk around him and pull the coffee out of the cupboard.

Ben leans against the counter as I make coffee. "We can always go fishing later."

I shove the pot into the machine with more force than necessary. "No, I'm already up. Let's do this."

"Whatever you say." He lifts his shoulder in an almost passive dismissal. "Where's Lucy?"

"I'm right here." Lucy comes out of the bedroom wearing sweats and an oversized hoodie. "Morning, Ben."

"Morning." Ben's gaze drifts between Lucy and me.

I smooth my hand over the front of my pants before turning toward her. "I forgot, Ben and I are going fishing this morning."

"You forgot?" Her gaze drops down the length of my torso then back up. "You must have been drunker than you thought. I heard him remind you before he went to bed last night."

Lucy brushes against me as she leans in to grab her coffee mug sitting on the counter by the coffee pot. "Excuse me." Her hip grazes my erection.

I bite my tongue and clench my hands into fists to keep from reaching for her. She grins when she turns and pushes me away.

"You're blocking the coffee."

I stare at her in disbelief.

"Want me to leave you two alone?" Ben cuts in.

"Why don't you go annoy your wife?" I glare at him,

ignoring the amused expression and his persistent grin. "I'll meet you at the dock in fifteen minutes."

"You sure that's enough time?" Ben jokes as he retreats toward the door.

"Get the fuck out!" I shout, wishing I had something to throw at his head.

Once the door closes behind him, laughter bubbles from behind me. I spin to see Lucy doubled over, tears running down her face.

"Ha ha. I'm glad you find my pain amusing." My side and my ego now show signs of bruising. I stalk to the coffee maker, pour myself a cup, and snatch the creamer from the fridge.

I sip my coffee and watch her struggle to compose herself. After a few moments, she straightens and wipes the tears from her eyes.

"Aww, you poor thing." She steps toward me, and I brace myself against the counter. "Does it hurt?"

"What? My dick?"

She smirks. "No, your pride."

"What pride? I'm supposed to be among friends." I scoff. "Some friends you all turned out to be. Laughing at a man in pain."

Lucy presses her hand to the center of my chest, palm flat. "Does it hurt that much?" Her hand drifts slowly down over my bare stomach. The muscle contracts beneath her touch, and I suck in a breath.

"Don't tease me." My brain ceases to work the moment her fingers toy with the hem of my pants where they ride low on my hips. Just an inch lower, please. I hold my breath and pray.

The warmth of her touch disappears. Lucy takes a step back and picks up her mug.

As my brain lurches back to life, I stand, dumbfounded, staring at the only woman in the world who can simultaneously drive me insane with lust and irritation.

I set my cup aside and cross the distance between us. I

grasp her hips and pin her against the countertop.

"The next time you tease me, I don't care if God himself comes knocking on that damn door, I'm going to claim your mouth and then your body. Do you understand?"

Lucy's eyes widen, her breath catches in her throat, and she nods.

"Good." I step back and retreat into the bathroom.

Once inside, I close the door and lean against the sink. My reflection seems no different than any other day, but I can see the tension simmering beneath the surface.

And I'm pretty sure Lucy can now too.

Ten minutes later, I'm out the door heading for the dock. Ben's already on the boat waiting. I climb in, and we shove off.

The sun's rays shine through the trees, reflecting on the water when we cast our first lines out. I feel the tension start to ease from my shoulders as I wait for a bite.

"What happened?"

I should have anticipated Ben's question. We're friends, and I knew he wouldn't be able to let it go.

"Nothing happened." I slowly reel in my line hoping the fish will take a nibble.

"Well, I know you didn't have sex. But something must have happened."

I glare at him. "Can we fish?"

Ben smiles and turns away.

When I glance back at the cabin, Lucy is on the porch, and I can't help but imagine what would've happened if Ben hadn't shown up at the ass crack of dawn to go fishing.

Chapter Twelve
Antiques and Admissions

Lucy

June

Penelope and I take the car into town, leaving the boys to enjoy their fishing time alone. Ben suggested we check out the antique market outside of town.

Honestly, the reprieve is exactly what I need. The last few days in Evan's company has left me completely off-kilter. When we were in the city, I could escape in my work and avoid everyone, including him. But being here in unfamiliar territory has me questioning everything.

After a few wrong turns, we find the antique market off the highway outside of town. It's a massive industrial building with *Antique* written in gigantic red letters on the roof. I've never seen anything like it, but it seems this whole vacation has been a non-stop bombardment of new experiences.

"Oh, this looks like fun." Penelope turns the key off and pulls it from the ignition. "I haven't been to one of these in years."

"These are common in Pennsylvania too?" I gawk at her.

"Yeah, I believe there are a few in Jersey once you get away from Trenton and Newark." She stares at me. "Haven't you ever gone antiquing?"

I face the red door bearing the handwritten welcome sign. "Do I look like the kind of girl who goes antiquing?"

Penelope shakes her head and laughs. "No, but looks can

be deceptive. Come on, I know you'll love it."

Once inside, I sigh with delight at the cool air hitting my face, dispelling the humidity. Then I see the rows and rows of junk. That's the only word I can find for it. Junk. If I bought a house with all this shit in it, I would haul it to the dump without a second thought.

"Let's explore." Penelope waves to the woman working behind the counter as we venture into the chaotic mess.

My head hurts from the visual overload. The rows, I realize, are organized into booths, and each booth contains a unique variety of junk spanning decades. I mean, VHS tapes, clothing, military gear, old kitchen supplies like pots and pans, glassware, the list goes on and on. I can't possibly be expected to look at every item in this place. It's physically impossible.

I watch Penelope drift lazily through the carnage, picking up objects and inspecting them before placing them back on the shelf and moving on. It's as if she's taking a leisurely stroll through Central Park rather than sorting through other people's unwanted, overpriced trash.

We venture deeper into the maze, and I start to see the pattern emerging. Among the typical odds and ends of garbage, an object catches my attention. One was a cast iron skillet. My mother uses them, and I've always wanted one. I pick it up and feel the weight of it in my hand.

"It's good for cooking and as a weapon," I joke and swing it like a bat.

"Hey, if it's good enough for Rapunzel, it's good enough for us, right?" Penelope laughs. "I mean she did use it to get herself a man too."

"Did we watch the same movie?" I grip the pan tighter as we move on through the building. "She knocked his ass out and stuffed him in a closet, then she threatened him with her frying pan and blackmailed him."

"But they fell in love." She points to a case full of jewelry.

"Oooh, pearls."

"That only happened because they were forced to spend time together." I glare at her as a slow realization hits me. "Penelope." I come up beside her as she drools over the pearl necklaces.

"What?" She doesn't look up.

I tug her arm with my free hand until she meets my eyes. "Did you set this whole thing up so I would spend more time with Evan?"

She shrugs.

"Penelope, tell me the truth."

Her shoulders slump. "Fine. Yes. It was a setup."

I drop my hand as the betrayal sinks in. "Why? I told you before, there's nothing between us. We're friends, end of conversation."

"But that's not true, is it?" She scowls, but Penelope looks more like a Brittany Spaniel than a Doberman, adorable and not in the slightest bit intimidating. "I saw the way you looked at him when you told me about what happened at the Christmas party."

"Really? And you're an expert on relationships now because you're happily married, right?" Bitterness laces the words, and I regret them as soon as they leave my tongue.

Penelope draws back as though I've slapped her. Hurt reflects in her eyes. "I wanted to help." She drops her gaze to the jewelry. "I'm sorry. I should've been honest with you." She draws herself up and boldly meets my gaze. Tears glitter in her eyes. "But you should learn to be honest with yourself, Lucy."

"What the hell does that mean?" Regret and anger mingle in the pit of my stomach making me nauseated.

She scoffs. "You have no idea do you? How much he cares?" Her gaze softens. "Evan loves you, Lucy."

Up until this moment before hearing the words aloud, I

was able to convince myself it wasn't true. There's no way. I buried myself in work and avoided him at every possible avenue. I fortified my walls and pushed him away with sarcasm and indifference. Why would he love me? How could it even be possible? He hardly knows me, and even if he did, it would never last. It never does.

"No." I shake my head fervently. "We barely know each other."

"Well, it's not like he hasn't tried taking the time to get to know you." Penelope's gaze softens. "Honey, he's been trying to get your attention for months. Haven't you noticed?"

I move on to the next booth, pretending to inspect the china on the shelf.

"Does Evan really make you uncomfortable?" Penelope asks, drawing up beside me. "I know he can be a bit much sometimes with the teasing and jokes, but he's a giant teddy bear."

"I know. I know." I groan. "No, Evan doesn't make me uncomfortable. In fact, it's more the opposite. He's sweet and charming and thoughtful. Being with him is too comfortable."

"That's a bad thing?" She arches her brows in surprise.

"Do we have to discuss this now?" I avoid her gaze and search the contents of a booth filled with handmade jewelry and metal sculptures.

"Yes, because I know you, and if I bring it up later, you're going to shut me down." She pins her hands on her hips and blocks my path.

I smile at her tenacity. "When did you get so bossy?"

"Last year." She grins. "Meeting Ben taught me one very valuable lesson. If you want something, you have to work for it. Why do you keep pushing Evan away?"

"I've told you before, I don't do relationships." I run my fingers across the glass case. "Am I attracted to Evan? Yes.

Did I sleep with him? Yes. Do I enjoy spending time with him? Yes. But that doesn't mean I'm ready to jump into a relationship or, heaven forbid, marry him."

"Look, I know we haven't been friends long, but I think of you like a sister. I only want what's best for you. You did the same thing for me last year when I was all twisted up about Ben, remember?"

I laugh. "It was a shit show."

"It wasn't that bad." She sniffs and smothers a smirk behind her hand. "Okay, fine. The boy was a train wreck." Penelope jabs me in the arm. "But you're not faring much better than he was."

"You're not helping."

"Okay. I'm sorry I dragged you to Middle-of-Nowhere, Indiana, and tricked you into staying in Evan's cabin and spending time with him. But can you tell me honestly you're not enjoying yourself even a little bit?"

My mind flicks through the events of the last few days, and I resign myself to the truth. "No. I mean, while it hasn't been a week on the white sand beaches with Mai Tais and cabana boys, it hasn't completely sucked. Although, it has been full of surprises. The 'possum, the storm, the tree, a day with his family."

"Visiting the in-laws is always an adventure. Ben and I spent the day with his family yesterday. That was an event and a half, let me tell you."

I laugh. "At least I wasn't alone."

"Well, you won't be on Saturday either."

The blood drains from my brain. "Wait, what? What's on Saturday?"

"Shit. I didn't tell you." Penelope chews her lip. "The boys thought it would be fun to invite their families to the lake on Saturday. A whole day of fun in the water and a barbeque. The whole nine yards."

"Fuck, Penelope." I close my eyes and take a few deep breaths. "You know I hate shit like this. Family events. Parties. It took all of my effort not to fall apart yesterday when I was in Evan's parents' kitchen surrounded by his sisters and his mom!" The panic creeps into my chest and squeezes my lungs.

"Breathe, Lucy." She rubs my back. "Just breathe. Deep breaths. That's it." We stand in silence for a moment until I'm able to wrangle the anxiety under my control again.

My fingers flex against the glass. Inside the case, a glint of silver catches my attention. The floundering panic fades into the background. I lean closer to inspect the pair of silver cufflinks on the top shelf of the case.

"Are you okay?" Penelope leans closer. "Do you need to step outside for some air?"

"No. I'm good." I stand up straight and face her. "I appreciate you wanting to help me. I know I'm not the easiest person to be friends with." I laugh. "I'm surprised you stuck around this long, to be honest."

"Aww." She hugs me with such force I stumble back against the case. "I love you, Lucy."

"I love you too."

"And whatever you want, I'll do my best to support your decision. No more matchmaking from me. Promise." She crosses her heart with her index finger.

"Good." I jab my finger at the case. "Now, who do I have to talk to about getting something from this booth?"

EVAN

JUNE

By three o'clock in the afternoon, Ben and I have a five-gallon bucket full of crappie, bass, and blue gill. It's enough to feed the four of us and then some, but I always enjoyed leftover fish when mom fried it.

Tonight, though, Ben and I are frying fish for the girls. I doubt Lucy has ever had fresh fried fish. Does she even like fish? I debate on asking Ben but decide against it since he's still harassing me for the state he found us in this morning. I don't need to give him another perfect opportunity to point out my shortcomings.

We're halfway through cleaning the fish when the girls return from their trip to the antique market. They join us once they put their purchases inside their respective cabins.

When Lucy approaches, she wrinkles her nose. "What are you doing?"

"Cleaning fish, what's it look like we're doing?" I toss a cleaned filet into the bowl.

"Making a God-awful mess." She frowns as she watches us work.

"Do you like fish?" I ask, curiosity getting the better of me.

"Not anymore." She waves her hand. "I'm going to get a drink. You guys want something?"

"Oh, let's make margaritas." Penelope takes her arm and drags her back to Ben's cabin.

I watch them until they disappear and catch Ben staring at me. "What?"

He shakes his head and continues boning fish filets.

A few hours later, after the fried fish is gone and the margaritas have kicked in, we take our seats around the fire pit as the sun dips beyond the horizon. Ben and Penelope sit across the fire, huddled close together on the loveseat bench. Lucy lounges in the Adirondack chair beside mine. Her attention consumed by the flames.

"How was the market?" I take a sip of my beer and admire the setting sun playing across her features.

"It was interesting." She smiles. "Took me a while to figure it out. Looked like a whole lot of junk shoved in a warehouse."

"Well, you're not wrong there." I laugh. "Did you find anything worthwhile?"

"A few things. Picked up an iron skillet." Her smile illuminates her face. "I always wanted one."

"I'm surprised you know what an iron skillet is?" I tease.

She glances at me in exasperation. "I may be a city girl, but I'm not an idiot. My mom had one when I was growing up. Used it almost every meal."

"I'm impressed."

"Plus, it doubles as a weapon. Sturdier than a baseball bat against intruders."

I choke on my beer mid-swallow and gape at her. "I pity the crook who tries to break into your place."

"Well, I know where to swing so it won't kill them, just break a bone or two." She chuckles and takes another sip of her drink.

"How many of those did you have?" I point to her half-empty margarita glass.

"Doesn't matter. I'm not driving anywhere."

"No, but I don't need you puking all over my cabin." I pass her a water bottle from the cooler beside me. "Do one and one."

"Are you always this overbearing?" She snatches the water from my hand.

"Are you always this stubborn?" I sigh. "I'm looking out for you. Hangovers in your thirties aren't like hangovers in your twenties."

She twists the cap and takes a drink. "Yeah, I know. It's been one of those days."

"Yeah. I feel ya there."

Penelope asks me a question and the four of us fall into an animated discussion about the marked differences of city versus country life. I can't keep my gaze from drifting to Lucy. Her vehement defense of city life slowly relaxes as we discuss the merits of both growing up in the city and the country. Unfortunately, it's three to one in favor of the country upbringing.

"Fine. We'll agree to disagree." She throws her hands up and stands, wobbling on her feet. "I'll be back."

I watch, torn, as she makes her way toward the cabin. Ben and Penelope stare pointedly.

"Go after her." Penelope mouths and jerks her thumb in the direction of my cabin.

"Shit." I dart across the lawn and take the steps two at a time. Once I'm inside the cabin, I pause at the sound of water running in the bathroom, and a thousand thoughts flood my mind.

Over the past nine months, I haven't been able to think of any woman but her. Even with our personality differences, I still find myself drawn to her passion and unabashed honesty. If only she would be honest with me about the one thing weighing on me without relief. There will never be a perfect time to ask her, so I take a deep breath and plunge headfirst into the storm.

The bathroom door opens. Her gaze snaps up, and a lazy smile graces her full lips. "Bathroom's free." She steps aside.

I close the gap between us. Her eyes widen.

"Lucy, I want to ask you a question." I lick my lips, and irrational fear grips my throat. "And I want you to be honest with me."

"Honest about what?" Her voice trembles.

"The Christmas party." I take a breath and push through. "Do you really think it was a mistake?"

She drops her gaze to the floor. "Evan."

"Just tell me the truth. Do you think what happened between us was a mistake?" I reach out and tip her chin up. Those soulful eyes draw me in, and I know no matter what she says, that night will always mean something to me.

"Yes." She stills beneath my touch. "For a while, I did."

"Did?" I brush my thumb across her jaw. "Past tense."

"Yeah." She scoffs and pushes my hand away.

"So there's hope." I prod gently knowing she's only seconds from pushing me away again.

Lucy shakes her head in exasperation. "You don't know when to give up, do you?"

I pin her against the wall, my hands on either side of her hips, our bodies inches apart. Her breath quickens. "If I gave up that easily, do you think I'd still be friends with Ben? Or have a successful business?" I cock my head. "It's not in my nature to run from a challenge."

"Is that all I am to you? A challenge?"

"No, sweetheart." I let my gaze drop to her lips. "You're not a challenge. Proving that this pull between us is worth pursuing has been the challenge, and one I gladly accepted because it would give me more than one night with you." I lean close and brush my lips against her ear. "Because you're worth more than one night of passion, Lucy. You're worth so much more."

Her breathless gasp makes me smile. I pull back enough to see the heat flicker in her gorgeous eyes.

"Did you practice that speech?" She rubs against me and the friction brings my cock to full attention.

"No." I grip her hips tight.

"Evan." Her lips hover over mine. "Finish what you started this morning."

Fuck. I pull her against me and cover her mouth with mine. She's sweeter and softer than I remember. Her body melts against me, and I deepen the kiss wanting all the passion she's willing to give. Her hands roam along my back, down until they grab the hem of my shirt and tug.

We stumble into the bedroom grasping at each other's clothes, tossing them in every direction until there's nothing between us but heat and desire. I draw her against me and kiss a trail down her throat, across the delicate curve of her shoulder. Her nails dig into my skin when I rake my teeth over her flesh.

"You taste so good." I murmur endearments against her body as I explore it with my tongue.

"Evan." She pants and pulls at my hair when I drop to my knees. "Please."

"You should know, I haven't touched anyone since that night." My confession cuts through the heavy air.

"Me either." She threads her fingers through my hair, and our eyes meet.

With a growl, I climb to my feet and pull her in for a fierce kiss, plundering her mouth, punishing her for months of torment. We stumble back and fall onto the bed, tangled in each other's arms, needing more contact. More everything.

A gentle vibration followed by strains of music fills the room. We both go still.

"Is that your phone?" I sit up.

Lucy climbs from the bed and grabs the phone from her discarded clothes. "Let me turn it off..." She goes still under the illumination of the screen. "One second."

She answers the phone. "Mom? It's after ten, what are you..." Her eyes widen and her jaw drops open. "Shit."

Fear slams headfirst into my gut. Something happened. I sit up and lean close.

"Mom, calm down. Where are they?" Lucy tucks the phone against her shoulder and continues talking while she gathers her clothing. "Okay. All right. I got it. I'll make some calls and then call you back. I'll get the first flight back. Text me if anything changes."

I'm on my feet and dressing before she hangs up the phone. "What happened?"

Lucy ignores me as she dresses.

I grab her shoulders and turn her to face me. "Lucy, talk to me. Let me help you."

"I need to get back to Brooklyn. Now." Her eyes fill with unshed tears. "My brothers were in an accident."

"Shit." I pull on my shirt. "Get your things together. I'll call the airport and get you a ticket for the first flight to the city."

I pull out my phone and text Ben, then I call the airport. It's going to be a long night, but it's the least I can do to ensure the woman I love is exactly where she needs to be.

CHAPTER THIRTEEN
WELCOME TO THE SHITSHOW

LUCY

JUNE

My mind spins as I disconnect the call with the hospital where my brothers have been admitted. My hospital. I'm part of one of the best trauma teams in the city. I trust them with my life, and now I have to trust them with my brothers' lives. I wipe the tears from my eyes. My brothers are in my fucking ER, and I'm not there. Damn it.

It's nearly midnight and we're halfway to Fort Wayne International Airport.

Evan stares intently at the road ahead. "What's the update?"

"Nick and Bobby are both alive and stable, but they're still critical." My voice cracks.

Without a word, Evan reaches over and takes my hand. It's a simple gesture of support, but it grounds me like nothing else. He squeezes tight.

"It'll be okay, Lucy. They're fighters, like you. In a few hours, you'll be there beside them."

I nod because I don't trust my voice. What if it's not okay? What if they die? What the fuck am I supposed to do? I should have been there.

A text message lights up my phone. It's Penelope.

Call me when you get to New York. I love you.

I smile and respond. *Love you too.*

Penelope helped me pack while Ben and Evan contacted the airlines to find the first flight heading to New York. The earliest they could find was six a.m. I took it. God knows when the next one will be, and I need to get home.

I lean my head against the glass and close my eyes. "You ever feel like your life is spinning out of control?"

"There's been a few times."

"I should be there. You know. At work. Helping my brothers." I don't know why I'm telling Evan any of this, but I need to vent or my head will explode.

"Guilt can be a tricky thing."

I scoff and blink away the tears.

"A few years ago, Ben and I had just started our company in New York, and all my time was dedicated to the business. I mean, I slept in my office half the time."

After wiping my tears with my sleeve, I glance at him.

He laughs. "I was almost as much as a workaholic as you and Ben." Evan sobers. "Then I got a call from my parents. Mom found out she had breast cancer, stage four."

"Evan." My heart constricts with sympathy and understanding. News like that is never easy, but being so far away makes it ten times harder. I take his hand and squeeze it.

"I felt like shit for months as she went through her treatments. I should've been there to help her and Dad. Even though I knew she had my sisters for support and a great team of docs helping her through the transition, the guilt consumed me." He clears his throat and laces his fingers with mine, pressing our palms together.

"She suffered through months of treatments and a double mastectomy, but she made it through. As you can see, she's fit as a fiddle now. Been cancer free for five years."

"I'm glad." Some of the tension seeps out of me as he tells his story. I know he's trying to tell me he understands and show support in his own way, and for that, I'm thankful. His words give me something to focus on other than my lack of control. "Why didn't you come home if you felt guilty for not being there for her?"

"She told me not to." He laughs. "Forbid me, actually.

Said I needed to get my company off the ground or I would regret it."

"Was she right?"

"In a way. Staying in the city to focus on the growth of the company benefited all of us in the long run. I used my first bonus to pay down her medical bills." He glances at me. "And as much as I wanted to be by her side as she fought for her life, I wouldn't have been much use hovering around the house feeling helpless. I couldn't fight the battle for her, no matter how much I wanted to save her from that pain."

Certainty settles in my chest. I know he's right. "That's true."

We pass a large green sign telling us to turn for the airport at the next exit. Evan takes the ramp, and my heart beats faster. I can't tell why. Is it the uncertainty of not knowing what's going on with my family? Is it leaving my friends behind? Guilt? Anxiety? A mixture of everything? I feel sick to my stomach.

Evan's thumb brushes over my hand. "Hey. It'll be okay. I promise. You're right where you need to be. There's no reason to beat yourself up for not being there. Okay?"

I nod, and a warm tangle of emotions twists in my chest. "Thank you, Evan. I appreciate it."

The lights of the airport come into view. I pull my hand away to gather my stuff together, and the loss of contact leaves me longing for something I can't examine right now.

He stops at the curbside drop-off for departures and turns off the car. There's not a soul around except for a security guard pacing inside the doors. As I gather my travel pillow and purse, he pulls my suitcase from the trunk and sets it on the sidewalk.

When he turns back from closing the trunk, I wrap my arms around him and bury my face against his sweatshirt. He holds me close, stroking my hair gently, telling me it will all work out. His scent calms me, his voice grounds me, if only for a few moments, I cling to him, knowing it's the only thing keeping me from falling apart completely.

"Do you want me to come with you?" His question warms my soul.

"No." I pull away enough to meet his concerned blue gaze. "Thanks though."

He hooks his thumb under my chin and tilts it up a fraction of an inch. "If you change your mind, I'm a phone call away."

My head bobs in acknowledgement, and my throat goes dry. I rise up on my toes and press a kiss to those sinful lips. Nothing passionate or desperate. A sweet exchange that leaves me breathless and aching.

"I—" The word brushes my mouth in a soft puff of air, but he stops short and smiles instead.

"Be safe. Text me when you land."

"I will. Bye, Evan." I grab my suitcase and wheel it toward the automatic doors. When I glance over my shoulder, Evan's leaning against the car watching me. He waves, and my conscience gives a strangle little lurch.

Quickly, I turn away and escape into the terminal.

It's not until I'm through security and waiting by my gate that I start replaying our goodbye in my head. I press my hand to my mouth, replaying the kiss over and over.

Finally, I shove it away. No, I can't think about it now. I can't bring myself to admit anything concerning my feelings for Evan, because if I do, then I will have to face my own past. And tonight, I don't have the fortitude to deal with the emotional fallout. I need to get home.

EVAN

JUNE

The hammer slams down on my thumb. "Fuck!" I toss the offending tool aside and storm into the kitchen to get a cold can of whatever's in there. I lean against the counter and press the ice-cold Coke to my throbbing finger.

"Evan?" Penelope peeks her head inside the door. She swings it wide when she sees me.

"Hey." I'm not in the mood for company, but I've never been able to tell Penelope no. Damn her sweet nature.

Ben follows behind his wife and closes the door behind them. I nod in greeting.

"Lucy made it to the city. She's at the hospital with her brothers." Penelope pulls out a chair at the table and sits down. "Just thought you'd want to know."

"Thanks. I'm glad she made it." Bitter bile burns the back of my throat. Even though I asked her to let me know when she made it home, I still hadn't received a text. She probably forgot. I ignore the other possibilities because I can't chase that rabbit, not today.

"What happened to your hand?" She points to the Coke I have pressed against my thumb.

"Hammer got me."

Ben scoffs. "I thought you were going to let the Amish fix the roof."

"I am." I frown. "But I still have to fix the damn bed. Frame broke."

"Want a hand?" Ben offers.

"Yeah. That'd be nice."

"What happened with you and Lucy last night?" Penelope's eyes glitter in the morning light, mischievous and excited.

I exhale a frustrated breath. "Why are you so concerned about what happens between us?"

Penelope looks as though I've slapped her. She bristles. "Excuse me for wanting to see two of my closest friends find happiness with each other."

"You can't force something to happen between us." I run my free hand over my face.

"No one's forcing anything between you two." She shoots to her feet and waves her arms around. "Watching you two together is like watching fireworks on the fourth of July."

She jabs her husband's side with her elbow. "Tell him."

Ben rolls his eyes. "She's not wrong. You two have been dancing around this for months."

"You guys are unbelievable." I replace the Coke and pull out a beer. Their eyes narrow on it before I crack it open. I don't give a fuck what time it is. "Just because there's chemistry and a history there, doesn't mean there's a future. So back the fuck off. Alright?"

Both of them stare at me stunned. Ben wraps his arm around his wife's waist and pulls her against him.

Penelope's lip quivers. "Evan, I know for a fact you love her. Why can't you admit it?"

"I admit it freely, but that doesn't do much, does it?" I take a healthy swallow of the brew.

"Did you say the words to her though?" Her eyes blaze and bore deep into my soul.

"I...fuck, I tried, but it didn't seem like the right time to tell her when she's about to board a plane to rush back to help her family with a medical emergency. She has enough to deal with without me throwing a curveball at her too."

"Lucy's a lot stronger than you give her credit for." Penelope crosses her arms.

"Why are you pushing this so hard?" I growl in irritation. "If it's meant to be, then fate will work it out, right?"

"Fate's doing a great job of setting you up for success so far," Ben chimes in with his signature lopsided grin.

"Fuck you. And fuck fate." I pound the rest of the beer and toss the can into the sink. "I have work to finish."

"Go after her. Tell her how you feel." Penelope's words make me pause in the doorway.

A fresh wave of frustration rises up and pulls me deeper into the darkness. "Life's not one of your fucking romance novels, Penelope."

She gasps, obviously hurt by my words, but I can't bring myself to care.

"Go outside for a minute. I got this." Ben shuffles his wife to the door.

Within moments of the door closing, Ben's closing in on me, his expression blank. He jabs his finger in my chest.

"You're lucky I know you well enough to know this isn't like you, because if anyone else had spoken to my wife like that, I'd break his jaw." Ben backs me against the door frame. The tone of his voice contradicts the unreadable expression on his face.

"Ben, I—"

"No excuses. You will apologize to my wife. She's done nothing but support and encourage you and Lucy, even though both of you are hellbent on making this harder than it has to be." His voice rumbles like a storm breaking the horizon.

"I was wrong to take it out on Penelope, but I can't keep playing this game." I shrug. "If Lucy doesn't want me, there's nothing I can do about it."

"Did you ask her what she wants?"

I stare, speechless, out the window to my right, unable to meet Ben's gaze.

"Maybe you should figure out what you want first, and then quit jerking around and go after it." Ben takes a step back, and I breathe easier knowing he's not going to hit me, even though he has every right to after the way I behaved.

"What if she doesn't want me?" I sound like a teenager pining over their first crush. It's almost cringeworthy.

"Evan. I've seen you charm politicians. I've watched you schmooze boardrooms and investors without effort. Hell, I've even seen you sweet talk a cop to get out of a parking ticket. A male cop, no less." Ben arches his brow. "And you're afraid of Lucy rejecting you?"

When he says it that way, my fear sounds ridiculous. But it doesn't make it any less real. I hang my head.

"We've taken a lot of risks, you and I." Ben rests his hand on my shoulder. "But we know the higher the risk, the better the reward."

"I know. But...fuck, Ben. I love her."

"I've heard you say those words before." He grins. "But

until this moment, I never believed it."

I shove him away. "You're not helping."

"Making you look at it is helping though, isn't it?" He heads to the front door and opens it, motioning for Penelope to come back inside.

There are red blotches on her cheeks. She sniffs and refuses to meet my gaze when she enters the room.

"Fuck, Penelope." I cross the room and pull her into a hug. "I'm sorry. I know you're only doing what you think is best for us. I was an asshole." I tip her chin up, and she meets my gaze with huge, sad eyes. "Will you forgive me?"

She steps out of my embrace and punches my shoulder. It catches me off guard and I stumble back. It doesn't hurt as much as it should, but I rub the spot for show.

"I should punch you in the mouth, jerk." She glares at me. "But then I'd ruin that pretty face for your reunion with Lucy."

"Penelope." I sigh. "She doesn't want me chasing after her."

"Are you sure about that?" She puts her hands on her hips.

"I told her to text me when she got home. I got nothing, but she messaged you." I shrug as though it's obvious.

Penelope rolls her eyes. "Men." She throws her hands up. "Fine. Wait a few days until you return to the city, then call her."

I glance at Ben, who nods in support of his wife. "You two are fucking relentless."

"You're welcome." Penelope beams. "Now, let's get this place back in shape before the party this weekend."

Ben and Penelope follow through on their offer to help me fix up the cabin. In the chaos of the past twelve hours, I'd forgotten about the massive family gathering at the lake this weekend. I give myself a mental shake.

A few days apart isn't the end of the world. I pull my phone out of my pocket and unlock the screen.

I type in a quick message and hit send, then I set the

phone on the table and return to the bedroom to finish repairing the bed fame.

Chapter Fourteen
Face the Music

Lucy

July

It's after six p.m. by the time I stumble into my apartment and collapse onto the couch. It's been a week since I got that terrible call about Nick and Bobby. A week since Evan and I...no, no, I'm not going there. Not now. Not ever. I can't. It hurts too much.

Since I returned to the city, I spent every waking moment at the hospital, which isn't different from my normal routine, honestly. Only this time I wasn't there working, I was hovering over my brothers' bedsides. I'm exhausted. Mentally and physically, I'm fucking drained.

My phone vibrates. I pull it from my back pocket. A text from Penelope. *How are you?*

Hanging in there, gonna take a nap. Talk later. I hit send.

Evan's unread message lingers in my inbox. I'm tempted to open it. The damn thing has been sitting there since the day I returned to the city. I could lie and say I forgot to reply in all the confusion, but it wouldn't be the truth. No, the truth terrifies me, and I'm too damn stubborn to face him or these heart wrenching emotions spinning inside me.

The intercom buzzes twice. I groan and peel myself off the couch to answer the call.

"Who is it?" I snap, not caring who it is at this point. I want to be left alone.

"Joey. Open the door, Lucy." His voice crackles through the intercom. "Don't make me play the welfare card."

I press the button to unlock the main door, and a minute later, there's a pounding on my apartment door. Without preamble, I swing it open.

"What do you want, Joey? I'm tired. I haven't showered yet. And you should know better than to show up without any..." I catch sight of the bag in his hand. Nino's subs. I glare at him and snatch the bag out of his hand.

He's still wearing his uniform pants and a plain button-down shirt.

"You just get off shift or what?" I plop the bag on the table and grab two plates from the cabinet.

"Nah, sat in court all day. Had to testify." He pulls two cold beers from the fridge and sits down across from me at the small kitchen table. "You work today?"

"No. I go back to work next week." I unwrap the Italian sub and my stomach growls at the scent of meat and spices. "I sat with Nick and Bobby all day."

He chews the bite of meatball sub and nods. "Yeah, I heard they're doing better."

"At least they're out of the ICU. Doc says they're recovering well."

"What do you think, nurse?" He grins knowing full well I have my own personal opinions on anything concerning medical needs and my family.

"I made a few suggestions to the attending and the nurses on duty." I smirk. "There are benefits to having them in my hospital."

"Mom stop by?" Joey licks the marinara off his fingers.

"Yeah, she sat with us for a while, had lunch, and then went home. Tonight's bingo at the center, remember?" It shouldn't bother me that Mom fell back into her routine so quickly after the accident, but it does. Joey knows it.

"You can't expect her to sit on her ass and do nothing at home. She can't sit in the hospital with them all day and all night. What's she supposed to do, Lucy? Huh?"

"They nearly died!" I snap and bite into my sandwich with a ferocity that leaves a spray of veggies over my plate.

"Yeah. They did." Joey wipes his hands off with a paper towel. "But you can't stop living just because bad shit happens!"

I scowl and toss the sub down onto my plate. He's lucky I have a mouthful of food, because I really want to let him have it. By the time I swallow, the rage dims.

"What the hell is that supposed to mean?"

He holds my gaze steadily. "This isn't about Nick and Bobby and the accident. Hell, it's not about Mom either, and we both fucking know it."

"Don't." My stomach lurches and bile stings the back of my throat.

"You've been busting your ass for years. Working eighty hours a week. Pulling night shifts, picking up every holiday you can." He picks up his beer. "Avoiding family events and your friends."

My mouth opens and shuts twice. I bite my tongue and take a drink to ease the burn of guilt.

"Is this what you want out of life? You want to work yourself into an early grave?"

"I love my job, and I'm damn good at it. Don't make this into something it's not." I face him down.

His expression softens. "Lucy, no one's saying you're not a great nurse. Hell, you're the best I've ever met, and I've met a lot of them over the years." He takes my hand and squeezes, just like Evan did in the car the last time we spoke. "But I'm worried about you. You deserve to be happy. Take up a hobby. Join a class. Go on a date. Hang out with your friends."

"I did that." My head aches at the memory.

"I'm proud of you for doing it. I know it wasn't easy for you to step outside your comfort zone."

"But look what happened when I left. Everything went to hell." I want to throw something, instead I nurse the beer and scowl.

"You think you're so powerful?" Joey laughs. "What the hell would you have done if you'd have been here when the accident happened?"

I groan. "Nothing."

"That's right. Not a damn thing. Because you know they wouldn't have allowed you in the room when they treated your brothers."

"I know. Damn it. But—"

"But what?" Joey leans forward dangling the beer from his fingertips. "Tell me you didn't enjoy your little trip to the sticks?"

His words conjure an image of Evan in my mind and my whole body warms. Shit.

"I thought so."

"What?" I bristle at his comment. "I didn't say anything."

"You didn't have to. Your face is red as pickled beets." He chuckles. "Doesn't take a detective to figure it out."

"Figure what out?"

"Come on, you really think I'm blind. You and Evan. I saw the looks you two were shootin' at each other back in May. Figured there'd be fireworks by now."

I scoff. "Whatever."

"You tellin' me nothing happened?"

"What's it matter to you if something happened?" I wave my hand and take a drink.

"You're my sister, and I want you to be happy." His simple response caught me off guard. "Evan's a great guy. He deserves a chance."

"A chance to do what?"

"To make you happy."

"I am happy."

"Sure you are." Joey sees straight through my lie. "Look, not all guys are lying, cheating, self-absorbed assholes like Doctor What's-His-Name. Evan is different."

I bristle at the reminder of my past and shake my head. "I don't want to talk about it."

I'm on my feet and halfway across the room when Joey's words make me pause.

"Just remember, if you keep pushing people away, you're

gonna die a lonely old maid with a shit ton of regrets." He drops his garbage into the trash and puts the plate in the sink. "See ya later, Lucy."

When the door closes behind him, I lean against the wall. His words echo in my head, and I want to claw them out and burn them to ash. For years, I played it safe. Everything was on my terms and my time. Joey knew about the asshole who ruined me, but only because he was the one who came home on military leave to find me broken and adrift. No one else knew because I never said a word.

Twelve years ago, I let a man make a fool of me, and I vowed it would never happen again.

After a quick shower, I clean up what remains of my dinner and tumble into bed. I glance at my phone sitting on the nightstand.

I sigh and grab it. In messages, I open Evan's conversation.

I miss you. Sent one week ago.

Another message dated four days ago.

I'm back in the city. We need to talk.

Anxiety curls in my chest, threatening to expand and consume me.

Yeah, we do. I hit send and clutch the phone to my chest. Maybe it's time I stop running away and face the truth that's been staring me in the face since Christmas. I'm in love with Evan. I only hope I haven't fucked things up beyond repair.

EVAN

JULY

Holy shit. I stare at the phone. She actually responded. I read the message twice before it hits me.

I type out a reply.

Now?

Three dots appear and disappear for a few moments.

Relief fills me when a response finally comes through.

My place. Two seconds later she sends a map pin with her location.

I'll be there in 30. My heart races as I reply.

Honestly, after a week of silence, I didn't expect to hear from her at all. It depleted my reserve of strength to keep from going to the hospital to check on her brothers and see her there. Hell, I'd even sent a message to Joey when I got back to the city just to make sure she was doing okay.

After grabbing a few things, I slip on my shoes and head out of the apartment. Thirty-five exhausting minutes later, I'm at the door of her building. Anticipation makes my heart pound and I wipe the sweat from my face. Well, it could've been from the pace I kept to get here in a decent time.

I press the buzzer and wait. A second later the door unlocks. I take the steps two at a time until I reach number nine. Before I can knock, the door swings open.

Words fail me when I see her. Even with a paint-stained tank top, mesh shorts, messy bun, and no makeup, she's never looked more beautiful. I grin when she smiles.

"Hey."

She crosses the threshold and grabs a handful of my shirt dragging me into the apartment, slamming the door closed behind me.

"Lucy, I..."

Her lips cover mine. The kiss steals my words along with any rational thought. I pull her against me and devour her mouth. Oh, God, how I missed her.

She clings to me as I stumble through the small living area. I nearly trip over the sofa and catch myself before we both fall.

"Lucy, baby, wait." I break the kiss to find my bearing and sit on the arm of the sofa with her pressed against me, her wide eyes burning with hunger.

Her hands press against my chest as she sobers and pulls away. "Sorry."

I snatch her hands and drag her back into my arms. "Hey.

Look at me." She meets my gaze. "I'm all for finishing what we started, but I'd like to do it without a trip to the ER."

Lucy laughs. "Good point." She grabs my hand and leads me into the bedroom.

Once inside, she releases my hand and pulls her tank top over her head, tossing it aside. No bra. I shake my head. Her breasts bounce as she pulls off her shorts, and those perfect nipples tighten, begging me to taste them.

"You gonna stand there and stare, or are you gonna strip?" Lucy steps closer and pulls at the hem of my shirt. With her help, I'm naked in less than a minute, basking in her touch as she runs her hands across my abdomen and over my hips.

"I missed you so damn much." I gasp when her fist closes around my cock. "Fuck." My grip on her tightens as she strokes me.

It's been too long and the sweet torture of her touch sends me too close to the edge. I push her back onto the bed and climb over her, nestling between those soft thighs. Once I've sated this beast, I'll enjoy her slowly, but right now I'm too far gone with lust to take it slow.

"You have protection?" I murmur against her neck in between kisses.

Lucy gestures to the box on her nightstand.

I fumble with the box before pulling one out. Her gaze follows me as I open one and slip it on.

"What do you want, sweetheart?" I tease her entrance.

"I want you." She thrusts her hips against me. "All of you."

"I'm all yours." I guide myself inside her tight heat and groan at the bliss of being sheathed inside her. I bury my face in her neck and take a deep breath. "Shit. You feel so fucking good."

When I lean back to drink in the sight of her, my heart sings at the sight of Lucy's glow, her cheeks pink, lips parted, eyes glazed with need. I thrust and her moan echoes off the walls.

She wraps her arms around me and rakes her fingernails across my back. Her hips rock in rhythm with mine. The bed sways beneath us creaking and thudding against the wall, but we're too far gone to care.

I roll onto my back. Lucy readjusts and takes me deep, riding me in slow, steady motions. My hands grip her hips, keeping her steady so I can watch the heat bloom across her skin and into her cheeks as the passion grips her tighter. When I press my thumb against her clit, she bucks harder and collapses forward, bracing herself against my chest.

Our eyes lock and I make tight little circles with my thumb. Every revolution drives her higher and higher. She licks her lips, soft moans pouring from between them. I rise up and kiss her, tasting the sweetness and swallowing every sound.

When she comes, her whole body goes stiff in my arms, her mouth gasping against mine. I push myself harder into her until I feel my own release teetering on the brink. Finally, it hits me and a wave of pleasure rolls through me, pulling me under.

She collapses against my chest and I hold her, content in the aftermath of months of pent up sexual need. I brush her hair away from her face and kiss her forehead. She nestles against me and kisses my chest.

"I love you." The words leave my lips without thought. Their effect echoes with truth down to the depths of my soul.

Lucy rolls off me and sits on the edge of the bed with her back to me. "I know."

I sit up and put my hand on her shoulder. "Are you okay?"

She turns to face me, tears pool in her eyes. "No. I'm not. I don't know what I'm doing, Evan."

"Hey, it's okay." I pull her against me and cradle her against my chest. "We can figure it out together." Her tears leave cool streaks against my skin. "Tell me what's going on in your head. What are you scared of?"

"You." She sniffs. "The last time someone told me they

loved me, I believed him. It ruined me." Her head shakes frantically. "I refuse to go through that again."

"Take a breath." I tip her chin up until our eyes meet. "Inhale." She takes a deep breath. "Exhale." It releases in whoosh. A shaky smile reaches her lips. "Better?"

She nods.

"Let's get something to drink. Okay?" I get up and grab my shorts.

Lucy slips on her clothes, and I follow her into the living room.

"Sit down. I'll get some water." I cross to the kitchen and try three cabinets before I find the glasses. Once I fill them, I join her on the couch.

"Thanks." Lucy takes a sip and settles back against the cushions. "I'm sorry."

"Nothing to be sorry for." I take a drink. "But if you want to talk, I'm here for you. How are your brothers?"

She brightens. "They're doing better. Not out of the woods yet, but definitely on the mend. Thank you."

"I'm glad to hear they're recovering. When do you return to work?"

"Monday."

"I bet you're excited to get back to doing what you do best, huh?" I smile hoping to encourage her to relax.

"I am." She fidgets with the glass in her hand. "Evan, I owe you an apology."

"For what?"

"For being an asshole." She sighs and pushes her hair behind her ears. "I didn't give you a chance before, and I'm sorry about that."

"Apology accepted, but there's no reason to feel guilty about it. I know you must have had your reasons for keeping your distance."

"I had reasons, but they weren't good ones. I made up my mind a long time ago I didn't want to be involved in any relationships, especially anything long term."

"That's understandable." I weigh my responses carefully

before I speak. I doubt Lucy's ever been this vulnerable before, and while I'm glad she's opening up to me, it's painful to see her struggle.

She cradles the cup in her hands. "When I got my first nursing gig, there was a doctor who worked in the ER with me. He made me feel special, and I made the mistake of sleeping with him." Lucy winces at the memory. "Two years I wasted on him. I thought it was a relationship, but he had different ideas. I found out from a group of gossiping nurses he was engaged to one of the residents. It devastated me. I walked out. It was Christmas Eve."

"Shit. I'm so sorry, Lucy." No wonder she swore off relationships. I want to offer some form of support, my hand or a hug, but I don't want to break the intimacy of the moment.

"It made me stronger. Made me a better nurse. But the older I got, the more my family pushed me to find someone, to get married, to start a family. After a while, I got so overwhelmed that I took the holiday shifts to avoid spending any extra time with my family and friends. For me, work was easier than explaining why I wasn't seeing anyone."

"So Christmas when you went to the roof?" The connection clicks in my mind.

"Panic attack." Lucy laughs. "You know it's strange. I can take the stress and chaos of the emergency room, but if you stick me in a social setting during the holidays, I'm a fucking train wreck."

"Why didn't you tell me sooner?" I reach out and take her hand.

"It's easier to hide it and use work as an excuse."

"Does Penelope know?"

"She knows I hate holidays and social gatherings." Her fingers entwine with mine. "But the rest, no. Our friendship is still relatively new, and she's so sensitive, I didn't want her to worry."

"She's stronger than you think." I remember our confrontation the morning Lucy flew back to the city and smile. "I think she'd understand."

"Yeah, I know. It's just, I've kept it locked away so long I forget it's there until it hits me in the moment. It must sound stupid to you."

"Not at all." I kiss her hand. "Thank you."

"For what?"

"Being open with me." I set her glass aside and draw her against me. "Trusting me."

She relaxes in my arms and rests her head against my shoulder. "Evan."

"Yeah."

"Do you really love me?"

"Yeah." I don't hesitate as the truth bursts free. "I do."

"Good." She leans back and stares up at me. "Because I love you too."

Words aren't enough to describe my joy. I kiss her, soft and sweet, pouring all the affection I harbor for her into the action. This woman is a beautiful wreck with her tearstains and messy hair and complicated history, but she's mine and I love her dearly.

"You're an amazing woman, Lucy Mackewitz, and I'm a lucky man."

"Damn straight." Lucy kisses me again until I'm dizzy. "Now, let's go back to bed. We have six months of sexual frustration to work out."

"Well, with that bed of yours making such a racket, your neighbors are going to riot." I nudge her. "Pack a bag. We'll spend the weekend at my place."

"Under one condition." She puts her hand on my chest.

"What's that?"

"Tell me you love me again."

"I love you, Lucy." I swat her ass with my palm. "Now, go pack, I have plans for you."

"You've been making promises since the day we met."

"Yes, and I have every intention of fulfilling them." I growl. "Now hurry, before I bend you over this couch."

CHAPTER FIFTEEN
CHRISTMAS, TAKE TWO

LUCY

CHRISTMAS, ONE YEAR AFTER THE INITIAL HOOK UP

"Remember, if you need to get some air, go to the roof." Evan squeezes my hand and offers an encouraging smile. "Just friends hanging out. No expectations."

"Thanks." I turn to face the gigantic poinsettia wreath hanging on the door. "But I think I'm good."

Evan knocks on the door. My heart flutters knowing this strong, handsome man is by my side. Last Christmas, the idea of a party terrified me, but now I'm excited to spend time with my closest friends and celebrate the holiday. Big accomplishment for sure.

The door swings open.

"Lucy!" Penelope bursts out into the cold and wraps her arms around me. "I'm so glad you came." She pulls away with a smile and hugs Evan. "Thanks for coming, guys. Come on in."

We follow Penelope into the house. Holy shit. I think there are even more decorations this year than last. Every room has a fully decorated tree, lights adorn each archway, and there's even tinsel hanging from the ceiling. How Ben tolerates this much chaos, I'll never know. Then I remember Penelope told me the decorations were his idea.

"Joey and his date are here already." Lucy weaves around the furniture. "I've already had to warn them twice to keep their hands off each other." She rolls her eyes but giggles nonetheless.

I smother a laugh when I walk into the kitchen. Ben's wearing the ugliest sweater I've ever seen. Red and green with giant gold letters spell out. *I've been naughty!* And he's wearing the same flashing antlers from the year before. He smooths his hair back from his eyes with one hand. His signature goatee now a full-on beard.

"Don't say it." He glares at Evan and then me. "Whisky?"

"Of course." I can't help but smile. He looks ridiculous.

Penelope leans against him and presses a kiss to his now-bearded cheek. "I think you look amazing, love."

Ben pours the drinks and hands them to us. Then he passes one to his wife. He holds the drink up.

"To friends." Penelope toasts with a grin. How can I not drink to that?

"So, you finally got your stuff moved into Evan's place?" Penelope's dances with excitement. "We'll finally be neighbors!"

"Yeah, it's official." Evan takes my hand. "I finally have her all to myself."

"Did you propose to her yet?" Penelope leans closer. "Seal the deal, so to speak."

I tense, and Evan's hand remains a steady point of anchor. Penelope and I have discussed it, and even though she knows Evan and I are serious about our relationship, she knows I'm not quite ready for such a huge leap. She means well, I know, but anxiety still blindsides me.

"Lucy and I have talked about it, but right now, we're taking it slow." He rubs his thumb across my palm, and I relax against him. "I'll wait as long as it takes 'cause she's the only one for me." Evan leans down and kisses my forehead.

I cling tighter to his arm. "Thank you."

"Aww." Penelope practically squeals. "You two are so cute." She elbows Ben. "I told you it would all work out."

Ben rolls his eyes heavenward and mouths something before turning to his wife. "You're lucky I love you so much or I'd strangle you with silver garland."

She slaps his arm and turns to us. "If I'm found dead in the river before New Year's, you know who did it."

"It's always the husband." Evan chuckles.

"Or the wife," I add.

Ben grabs Penelope by the waist and kisses her thoroughly. I blush and turn to Evan, who seems disgusted by the display.

"Shall we?" Evan takes my hand and turns away from Ben and Penelope who look like they're two seconds from making love on the kitchen island.

I follow him through the house. He grabs our coats in the entry way and heads up the stairs toward the roof.

The city lights sparkle in the distance. A cold breeze wraps around us as we sit on the bench facing Manhattan.

Evan pulls me against him.

"Did you mean what you said?" I ask watching my breath curl in the cold December air.

"About waiting for you." He smiles and those blue eyes sparkle in the dim light. "Of course I did."

"I appreciate that. Really." I lean my head against his shoulder. "I'm sorry I'm not making this easy for you."

"You're worth it, Lucy." His voice rumbles through me and it soothes any lingering guilt.

We stare out over the skyline for a few quiet moments content in each other's company.

"I miss seeing the stars."

I glance up at him. He's searching the heavens overhead with a frown on his face.

"Yeah, it's hard to see the stars in the city. I never noticed until you showed me." I nestle closer to him absorbing his heat. "At least we still have the moon."

"And I have you." He tilts my chin up and kisses me. I melt against him.

He runs his hands down over my sides and drags me into his lap. The kiss deepens and I'm lost in the sensations spiraling down into a torrent of desire. I put my hand on his chest and break away.

"We shouldn't make this a habit." My voice is breathless. "Hooking up at our friend's Christmas party."

"I don't know. Sounds like a fun tradition to me." He wraps his arm around my waist beneath my coat and kisses my neck.

"Only you would think that." I laugh.

"Did you see them down there? They were about to get freaky right there in front of us." He arches his brows. "And Penelope said Joey was getting handsy with his date too. I don't know, maybe there's something in the whisky?"

"Oh, God. Can we please not talk about my brother getting handsy with anyone?" I gag at the mental image.

"Can we talk about me getting handsy with you?" Evan brushes his mouth against my throat.

"Later." I moan when he nips my skin.

"Talk later or get handsy later?" He chuckles.

"Both, maybe, I can't think when you tease me."

He draws my ear lobe between his teeth and pulls gently. "Good." He runs his hand along my outer thigh, up and over my hip. "What's this?" He presses his fingers against the lump in my pocket.

"Oh, I almost forgot." I readjust my seat on his lap and dig the small bag out of my pocket. "Merry Christmas."

He takes the small velvet bag from my hand and pulls the strings open. When he pours the contents into his hand, I hold my breath.

Two round silver cufflinks with blue gems glint in the dim light. He picks on up and peers closely at it. His eyes widen and shift to meet mine.

"I saw them and I thought of you."

"They're beautiful." He looks closer. "Is that Orion?"

"Yes. They're constellation cufflinks." I lean closer. "Do you like them?"

"I love them. They're perfect." Evan slips them back in the bag and tucks them into the breast pocket of his coat. "You're perfect." His kiss warms me to my toes. "Thank you."

"You're welcome." I wrap my arms around his neck.

He studies my face. "Where on earth did you find them?"

"The antique market."

He pulls back, surprised. "The one outside of Shipshewana?"

I nod with a grin.

"You've been saving them for a Christmas present?"

"Well." My face heats. "I mean, I've been meaning to give them to you for a while, but it seemed better to wait for the right moment."

"Did I ruin it?"

"Not at all. This is the perfect moment." I pull him closer. "I love you, Evan, even though you drive me crazy."

"The feeling is mutual." He slides his hand beneath my blouse. "Now, about that tradition."

And just like that, a holiday love affair came full circle.

THE END

CRAVING MORE?

READ A LOCKDOWN LOVE AFFAIR

BEN AND PENELOPE'S STORY

&

MISTLETOE AND MISTAKES

ANDREW AND VIVIAN'S STORY

OTHER BOOKS BY KIRSTEN S. BLACKETER

CRAVING 1985 SERIES
When I Found You
Can't Fight This Feeling
She Gives Love a Bad Name
Owner of a Lonely Heart
Just What I Needed

HISTORICAL
An Irresistible Shadow
A Shadow's Kiss
Mississippi Moonshine
Deceiving the Earl
Jewel of Winter
At Winter's Demand
Under Winter's Control
Seducing Winter's Gentleman
Stealing the Widow's Heart
Seduction on the Alpine Express
Temptation on the Alpine Express

CONTEMPORARY
A Lockdown Love Affair
A Holiday Love Affair
Mistletoe and Mistakes
Confessions of a Fangirl
Confessions of a Gamer Girl
Confessions of a Glamour Girl
The Flight Before Christmas

FANTASY/FAIRYTALE
Curse of the Huntsman's Jewel
The Huntsman's Revenge

PIRATES AND PERSUASION
Queen Takes Hook

ABOUT THE AUTHOR
KIRSTEN S. BLACKETER

Kirsten S. Blacketer is a multi-published indie author of both historical and contemporary romance. When she's not writing, she homeschools her two children and enjoys time with her family. In those moments of freedom, she devours romance novels while sipping a glass of wine. Age has only shown her that writing villains can be just as fun as heroes. Her next life goals are to write a New York Times Bestseller and one day have Adam Driver play a starring role in a film version of one of her books. A girl can dream, right?

Read more at **http://kirstensblacketer.com.**

ALSO WRITES AS JEN BRADLEE